Shannon
Thank you for sharing
in the adventures
of my childhood!
Enjoy the journey!

7-23-22

Big Clifty, Star Route

KENNETH R. POWELL

WESTBOW PRESS®
A DIVISION OF THOMAS NELSON & ZONDERVAN

This is a work of fiction. All of the characters, names, incidents, organizations, and dialogue in this novel are either the products of the author's imagination or are used fictitiously.

WestBow Press books may be ordered through booksellers or by contacting:

WestBow Press
A Division of Thomas Nelson & Zondervan
1663 Liberty Drive
Bloomington, IN 47403
www.westbowpress.com
844-714-3454

ISBN: 978-1-6642-6820-3 (sc)
ISBN: 978-1-6642-6822-7 (hc)
ISBN: 978-1-6642-6821-0 (e)

Library of Congress Control Number: 2022910686

Print information available on the last page.

WestBow Press rev. date: 6/21/2022

This book is dedicated to my high school English teachers. Elaine Alicna, Tommy Owsley, and Shannon Campbell taught me grammar and sentence structure, creative writing, and how to use the written word as an expression of the inner being. They also helped me gain a lasting appreciation for the great writers and their works. I would like to especially thank Mr. Campbell, who provided me with encouraging feedback on my first effort at a published work, "Twilight in Kentucky," which graced the cover of *SupeRx Drugs People* magazine. This book is also dedicated to my sister Mary, who challenged me to write this specific book. I also want to thank Chuck Mattingly for his editing and honest critique. Lastly, this book is dedicated to Bud, who allowed me to share the story.

Contents

Preface ix

No School Today 1
Hodge's Store 8
New Neighbors 14
Lights Out 21
Mom's Christmas Tree 26
Frozen, Stiff as a Board 29
Tobacco Bed 33
Good News/Bad News 35
Mayapples and Mumblety-Peg 38
Pop Bottles and Claire Marie 43
Looking Sharp 49
Striped Bass 53
Bud's Own Barlow 58
Do It Right or Go to the House 61
Polebridge Missionary Baptist Church 65
Arthur Ray's New Buick 70
Aunt Matt 72
Setting Tobacco 76

July Birthdays....78
Baptism Sunday....82
Big Six Henderson....86
Powell Family Reunion.... 90
Top, Sucker, and Prime....94
Hank's Bright Idea....96
Barn Raising.... 100
A Weekend in Eastview.... 104
Tobacco Harvest....111
Halloween Pranks....115
Lessons Learned....118
Black Thread and Pain.... 123
Commodities, Cats, and the U.S. Navy.... 128
Opal in Pink.... 136
A Christmas Present for Claire Marie.... 138

About the Author....141

Preface

The author grew up in the small community of Limp, Kentucky, with five brothers and two sisters. Like a lot of other kids in rural Kentucky, they experienced the pain of poverty. They also were blessed with drive and ambition to climb out of poverty. Education was the surest means to accomplish that. Their father pushed them in school and in life, with a work ethic that dictated, "To succeed in life, you kids must work longer, harder, and smarter than anyone else." After the siblings were grown and had families of their own, Mary encouraged her little brother (who is the writer in the family) to author this book so their children and grandchildren could get a taste of what their childhood was like. Some of the stories in the book are historically accurate. Some are loosely based on actual events. Some are completely fictitious, added only to help complete the story.

No School Today

"Wake up, Bud! Time to get up!"

Bud awoke to the sound of Mom's voice calling from the kitchen. Bud sat up in bed and rubbed his eyes. Faint light was already peeking through the bedroom curtains. Bud watched dust particles floating in the morning sun's rays. It was already daylight outside!

"Mom! What time is it? I'm going to miss the school bus!"

Bud loved school, especially reading. His cousin Peggy was a schoolteacher in Chicago. When she came down to Kentucky to visit, she usually brought along some decommissioned textbooks from her school. These included reading texts like *Singing Wheels* and *Engine Whistles,* which were set in the time frame of the late 1800s and early 1900s. Cousin Peggy had also brought a textbook for American history, which Bud had read several times. Bud hadn't missed a day of school since he started. He was in the fourth grade and wasn't about to miss school now!

"It's OK, son." Mom's voice was very calm. "Look outside."

Bud ran to the bedroom window and pulled back the curtains. Everything was covered in snow! Deep snow! The morning sun sparkled on the crusted snow. The wind was gusting out of the west, causing the snow to drift. In some places, the drifts were knee-deep already. Light clouds of snow were blowing across the backyard, and Bud could barely make out the barns. Bud rushed to get dressed, to go outside, forgetting all about breakfast. He pulled on two pairs of socks, his favorite Levi's jeans, and a fleece hoody over his T-shirt. A million thoughts rushed through his mind.

"Can I go outside, Mom? Where are Jimbo and Hank?"

Jimbo and Hank were Bud's older brothers. Jimbo was in his senior year at West Hardin High School. Jimbo wanted to be a mechanic like Pap. He was tall and muscular and as strong as an ox. Hank was just a year younger. Hank was not quite as tall as Jimbo and not quite as strong. Hank was really smart and had a knack for coming up with bright ideas on how to do things faster, easier, or just different for the sake of being different.

"Mom! Where are my five-buckle boots?"

"Slow down, Bud. Come in here and eat your breakfast. Your oatmeal is getting cold."

Mom made hot Quaker brand oatmeal every morning for Bud and his brothers. She said they needed something that would stick to their ribs, something that would last until lunch. Mom cooked on a gas stove powered by two propane tanks that sat just outside the kitchen window. "Foster Gas, Leitchfield, KY" was stenciled on the side of each tank in bright red letters. Beside the stove, Mom had a wall plaque declaring, "This is *my* kitchen. If you don't like it, Starve!" Bud never understood why Mom hung that plaque on the wall. She was a really good cook! So Bud never complained about Mom's cooking. He ate whatever she put on the table.

The table had a red top with chrome legs and chrome trim around the edges. The chairs were also chrome, with red plastic seats and backrests. Pap had bought the table used from his cousin Lloyd Powell up in Elizabethtown. Lloyd and his wife, Gladys, always kept the table covered with a fresh linen tablecloth so it looked brand new. Bud sat down at the end of the table next to the kitchen stove, and Mom placed a bowl of hot oatmeal in front of him. A dab of homemade butter and some cinnamon sprinkles on top—just the way Bud liked it! Bud stirred the steaming oatmeal, hoping it would cool off enough to eat quickly. A radio sat on the kitchen counter and Mom had it tuned to 840 AM, WHAS, in Louisville. Bud could hear the list of school closings county by county.

"Franklin, Grayson, Hardin, Jefferson ..."

Nope, no school today!

Bud gobbled down his bowl of oatmeal and drank his glass of milk. As soon as his feet hit the floor, he was headed toward the back door. Winter coat, five-buckle boots, toboggan for his head, and gloves for his hands. Time to go outside and play in the snow!

"Go help your big brothers clear a path to the barn. I need to milk the cows. And come in when your nose gets cold!"

"Yes, ma'am!"

Bud raced through the laundry room and out the back door. Jimbo and Hank were busy using scoop shovels from the corncrib to cut a path to the barn. Mom couldn't get to the barn because of the snowdrifts, and the cows Bessie and Little Bit were mooing and anxious. Bessie was a Jersey, and Little Bit was a cross between a Holstein and a Guernsey. Mom sat on a three-legged stool while she milked the cows twice a day. Between them, the family cows produced a couple of gallons of milk each day. There was always fresh milk in the Frigidaire. And sometimes homemade ice cream in the freezer!

The snow was almost up to Bud's waist as he headed down the snow path to help his brothers. Jimbo and Hank did most of the shoveling, but they let Bud help in places where the snow was not so deep. Bud really wasn't big enough to handle a corn scoop shovel, but he didn't want his brothers to think he was just a little kid.

In a couple of hours, they cleared a path to the barn for Mom. They met her as they were headed back to the house, with their scoop shovels thrown over their shoulders. Mom headed to the barn while carrying a milk bucket in each arm.

"Can we build a snow igloo in the yard?"

"Yes, boys. Just be sure not to dig up any grass. We do not want to leave the yard a mess come springtime."

Jimbo stomped out a circle in the snow, about six feet in diameter, just outside the kitchen window. Then he and Hank used their scoop shovels to cut square blocks of snow and began to arrange them around the circle. Each layer of blocks made a slightly smaller ring until a single block finished the top of the igloo. Bud's job was to use loose snow to fill in the cracks between the blocks, first on the outside and then on the inside.

Before long, the igloo was completed. The boys carried an old bale of straw up from the barn and used it to line the inside of the igloo, and they laid some empty burlap feed sacks on top of the straw bedding. Altogether, it made a comfortable floor.

Bud was surprised at how warm it was inside the igloo. And light too! Just enough sunlight filtered through the snow blocks to create a soft glow. The boys had a grand time all morning, pretending to be Eskimos in Alaska.

They completely lost track of time until they heard Mom's voice out the back door of the house, calling them inside for lunch. Pinto beans, with a slice of onion, and hot cornbread cooked in lard, fresh out of the oven. And of course, a glass of fresh, ice-cold milk for each boy.

"Eat up, boys. You will need some energy this afternoon. I need you to shovel out a path to the road, in case we need to get out. And Bud, I need you to walk to Hodge's Store and pick up a bag of sugar. We are about out of it and I don't know when we will be able to get to town. But be on the lookout for any traffic on the Salt River Road!"

Salt River Road was one of the oldest roads around. It ran from Leitchfield all the way to West Point, where the Salt River emptied into the Ohio River. Farmers from across central Kentucky used the road to haul livestock, lumber, and grain to load onto river barges at West Point. From there, those goods were transported to other regions of the country. In return, they were able to pick up coal, sugar, and the other products. The Salt River Road had been a major highway back in its day. Now it was just a good gravel road.

Jimbo, Hank, and Bud cleaned their plates, got bundled up again, and headed back outside to start shoveling the driveway. Only this time, shoveling was not as much fun. It was work.

After a couple of hours shoveling snow, their arms and shoulders were getting sore. By the time they shoveled their way to the mailbox, they were pretty well tuckered out. Thankfully, the wind had died down and the snow had stopped drifting. Otherwise, all their work would have been for nothing.

Their mailbox was huge—big enough to hold any catalogs or boxed packages. Pap had it mounted on a steel pipe set in a cream can filled with concrete. The previous mailbox had been blown up by some teenaged pranksters, so Pap built its replacement solid. Then next year, when those boys were blowing up the neighbors' mailboxes, they just blew open the door on this one. Bud pulled down the door on the mailbox and looked inside. The mailbox was empty. The mailman hadn't run yet. In fact, the Salt River Road looked like no traffic had been on it at all.

Jimbo and Hank headed back to the house. It had finally stopped snowing, and the sun was climbing in the eastern sky. Snowflakes on top of the snowdrifts sparkled in the bright sunlight. Bud squinted his eyes and peered up the

Salt River Road, searching for the best path up to Hodge's Store. Mr. Dewey Hodge and his wife, Ethel, owned Hodge's Store, which was at the center of the community of Limp, Kentucky. At one time, the post office operated from inside the store. But Limp, like a lot of other smaller communities around the state, lost its post office due to consolidation. Automobiles made it easier for the mail carriers to service a larger area out of one post office. Now their mail came from the post office in Big Clifty. Instead of picking up mail at Hodge's Store, it was delivered by automobile to the mailbox at the end of the driveway.

"Big Clifty, Star Route, Box 241." That was Bud's address.

Hodge's Store

Hodge's Store had a wide porch across the front of the building, where neighbors sat in rocking chairs in nice weather to swap stories and discuss politics and farming ideas. Inside Hodge's had hardwood floors and shelves filled with a variety of canned goods and bags of bulk kitchen items like sugar, flour, and cornmeal. The walls of the store were lined with hooks and nails, holding all kinds of general merchandise from shovels to milk buckets. A coal-burning potbellied stove dominated the center of the store. A small round table and four straight-backed, cane-bottom chairs sat in front of the stove. In bad weather, folks gathered around to be warmed by the stove. Sometimes they sat at the table and played checkers while Mr. Hodge pulled their orders.

A wooden countertop with a glass front ran all along one side of the store. Mr. Hodge kept special merchandise inside the glass display case. New dishes, bolts of material, and supplies like needles and spools of thread. Mom bought her thread from Mr. Hodge's store and used it to patch up most of their clothes. Once those clothes were beyond repair, she saved the scraps to make aprons or quilting squares. Mom always wore an apron, whether she was in the kitchen cooking, cleaning around the house, or working in the garden. Usually around back-to-school time, Mom would buy a yard or two of material from Mr. Hodge. She used her Singer foot-pedal sewing machine to make the boys new shirts cut from patterns she ordered through the Montgomery Ward catalog.

On top of the counter were candy jars and spinning glass displays with watches, jewelry, lighters, and pocketknives. Bud had his eye on those pocketknives. He dreamed of having one of his own someday. Most of the boys in the neighborhood carried Case pocketknives because that's what their dads carried. Bud was different. He was especially fond of the three-bladed Barlow with its brown bone handles. Sometimes, Mr. Hodge would get the Barlow out of the case and let Bud play with it.

Bud loved hanging around Mr. Hodge's store, and with Mr. Hodge himself. Dewey Hodge had been in the war and lost his right arm, to just above the elbow. Now he just had a stump for a right arm. Bud tried not to stare at Mr. Hodge's arm, but he couldn't help himself. He had never seen a one-armed man before. And Mr. Hodge took a liking to Bud, too. Dewey and Ethel Hodge never had any children, and Bud was almost like a son to them.

Visions of the inside of Hodge's Store danced inside Bud's head as he made his way up the Salt River Road toward the front steps of the store. He was glad to see smoke coming from the chimney and knew Mr. Hodge had a good fire blazing in the stove. He climbed the five steps up to the front porch and opened the screen door with its push bar declaring, "Colonial, It's Good Bread." Normally, the screen door was all there was to open, but in winter, Mr. Hodge kept the wooden door closed to keep the heat in and the cold out. Both doors squeaked as they opened and closed behind Bud.

Mr. Hodge spotted Bud from behind the counter. "Hey, Bud! What brings you out in this weather?"

"Mom sent me after a bag of sugar. She said with this storm, she's not sure when we'll get to town."

"OK, I'll get her a bag and put it on her tab. Here, enjoy a piece of candy. Your choice."

Bud peered inside each of the glass Lance candy jars on the counter. Gumdrops, licorice sticks, peanut butter logs, jawbreakers, chocolate-covered peanuts, and striped peppermint sticks.

"Can I have some of those peanuts?"

"Sure, help yourself."

Bud couldn't help but remember a funny story about those chocolate-covered peanuts. Mr. Hodge always kept a bowl on the counter for the customers to sample while he picked their bulk grocery orders from the sales floor or the back storeroom. Every morning, Knobby Auberry would walk up to the store after his morning nip of whiskey and stand at the counter munching on the chocolate-covered peanuts until the bowl was empty. Then he would say he had to be going and head back down the Salt River Road to his house. Mr. Hodge finally got tired of the freeloading and decided to break Knobby of this habit.

It happened last winter when a snow was on, almost as deep as this one. Knobby Auberry came into the store that morning as usual and ate all the chocolate-covered peanuts as usual. Except this time, Mr. Hodge had mixed in a box of Carter's Little Liver Pills, a powerful laxative. The pills were round and brown and looked a lot like chocolate-covered peanuts. That morning, after Knobby left the store, he climbed down the steps and made it just a few steps before he had to drop his pants in the middle of the Salt River Road. He left brown spots in the snow about every hundred feet between the store and his house.

Knobby didn't show up at the store for several days, and Mr. Hodge was getting a little worried about him. One morning, Mr. Hodge and Bud decided to walk down to Knobby's house to check on him. The fire had gone out in the stove in the living room, and Knobby's house was freezing cold. They opened the bedroom door to find Knobby curled up in bed, shivering under a pile of blankets and quilts. A chamber pot was sitting on the floor beside the bed, and it was overflowing. Knobby had diarrhea so bad he couldn't make it to the outhouse. He didn't even have the strength to keep the fire going in the stove.

"Come in here in the living room, Bud, and help me get a fire started."

Bud and Mr. Hodge found some kindling and loose paper and got a fire started. Bud went outside to the woodshed and brought in several armloads of firewood and stacked it beside the stove. Soon the house began to warm up. Mr. Hodge sat the chamber pot on top of the stove to thaw it out enough to be dumped outside. He told Bud to keep an eye on it so it didn't boil over. Mr. Hodge had a big enough mess to clean up in the bedroom. Finally, they got Knobby out of bed and dressed. Bud boiled some water for oatmeal and made some hot coffee on the stove. Knobby ate like a starved man and acted like he could take care of himself. Mr. Hodge reckoned they had done enough. Besides, there might be customers waiting at the store.

When they left Knobby's house, Bud could tell Mr. Hodge felt pretty bad about Knobby's condition. Mr. Hodge never said another word about the lesson he had taught Knobby. Knobby took a few days to regain his strength enough to walk up to the store. From that day forward, Knobby left the peanuts alone. Reckoned he had developed an allergy to peanuts, or something. Bud was thankful he wasn't allergic to peanuts. He sampled just a few while Mr. Hodge retrieved a bag of sugar from the storeroom and carried it cradled in his left arm.

"OK, Bud, your sugar is ready to go. Say hello to your mom and dad for me."

"Thanks, Mr. Hodge! And thanks for the peanuts, too!"

As Bud headed out the front door of Hodge's Store, he heard the road graders coming down the Salt River Road. He saw their flashing lights and waited on the front porch until the yellow road graders had passed. One was plowing snow to the left side, the other to the right. The result was a clear path down the middle of the road. Now Bud didn't need to wade through the deep snow to get home. He just had to watch for any traffic. But there wasn't any traffic. Nobody in their right mind would get out in this mess unless it was absolutely necessary.

When Bud got back to the house, Mom reminded him to check the woodbox behind the Warm Morning wood-burning stove in the living room. It was Bud's job to carry in the firewood and keep the woodbox piled high. Sure enough, the woodbox was a little low. Armload by armload, he carried in fresh wood until the box was full. The living room was filled with the warm smell of split oak firewood. The kitchen was filled with a different smell: freshly baked cornbread, brown pinto beans, and homemade apple pie! Mom called the family into the kitchen for supper.

After supper, Bud's eyes were already getting heavy. Today had been a day filled with hard work and adventure. It was going to be an early bedtime tonight. Any thoughts about going back outside would have to wait until tomorrow.

New Neighbors

Sometime in the middle of the night, Bud was awakened by a commotion in the living room. Somebody was pounding on the front door.

He heard Mom. "Pap, get up! There is someone at the door!"

When Pap bought the house, years ago, it was just two log cabins with a dog trot covered breezeway between them. Pap put a floor in the dog trot and framed it to create a bedroom between the living room cabin and the bedroom cabin. Later, he added three more rooms along the back of the house for a kitchen, a laundry room, and a third bedroom. Bud and his brothers slept in the back bedroom. Mom and Pap shared the middle bedroom, but mostly Mom slept on the couch.

Pap got hurt really bad building the back of the house. He had jacked up one wall to level it with the rest of the house. It slipped off the railroad jacks and landed on top of him. One of Pap's kidneys was torn and had to be removed. The doctors said he would be at risk the rest of his life. If something happened to his other kidney, it would kill him. So Pap had to quit his job as a mechanic. From that day, Pap was disabled so Jimbo and Hank had to do most of the heavy work on the farm.

Mom found the matches and lit the coal oil lamp to light the living room and added another stick of oak firewood to the Warm Morning wood stove. The wind had picked back up in the middle of the night and snow had drifted up against the front door. Mom pulled open the heavy front door and snow blew into her living room.

In front of her stood a strange man with a panicked look on his face. His ears and nose were bright red, and he was shivering from the cold. "You do not know me, ma'am, but I need your help bad. My name is Probus, and my family just moved into the Adams place down the road from the Dennis family. My wife is having a baby and we're on our way to the hospital in Leitchfield. We got the car stuck in a snowdrift trying to ford the creek. Have you got a tractor to pull us out?"

"Come on in, neighbor, and warm by the stove while Pap gets dressed and ready. I will fix you some hot coffee."

Mr. Probus pulled off his gloves and warmed his hands over the stove in the living room. Little by little, he stopped shivering.

"Your house sure is nice and toasty. I was beginning to wonder if I might get frostbite before I could wake someone."

The house really *was* toasty. In fact, it sometimes got too hot, even in cold weather. Mom might have to crack a window in the living room just a bit to keep the temperature under ninety degrees. The log walls were thick and well insulated so the wood stove heated the whole house very well. Mom returned from the kitchen with a hot cup of coffee for Mr. Probus just as Pap entered the living room. Pap had put on a thick, flannel shirt over his nightshirt then slipped into his winter insulated overalls and his five buckle rubber boots. Mr. Probus thanked Bud's mom for the coffee and began to sip it.

"Hello, neighbor. Welcome to our home. I'm Perci. Perci Albin Powell. Most people call me Pap. This is my wife, Roberta. I am glad you found us, and I am glad to help you out. Around here, neighbors are happy to help each other. That's what we do! Let me go warm up the tractor while you thaw out by the stove."

Pap headed out the back door toward the barn. Everyone did call him Pap. Although his initials were PAP, most people called him Pap because of his age. Pap was a lot older than Mom, about fourteen years. Bud had asked Mom once about that. Mom just said it was different for her, growing up. Her parents were well-to-do and each year hosted a square dance at their farm. All the prominent people in the community showed up. It was a real opportunity for match making. But Mom had other ideas.

Pap was a banjo picker in a bluegrass band that played the square dance one year. Pap was a handsome man with dark, wavy hair and wire-rimmed glasses. Mom was smitten, and when Pap asked her out on a date, she jumped at the chance. Mom's dad wasn't too happy about her choice in Pap. He wanted her to marry a doctor, a lawyer, or a well-to-do insurance agent. Any outstanding young man would be OK, so long as he was a Catholic. Pap wasn't any of those things. He was a banjo-picking mechanic. And he certainly was not a Catholic. No, her dad was not happy with Mom's choice in Pap, but she married him anyway. The newlyweds moved away to the country, far away from her parents and the Catholic church. Her parents disowned and disinherited her, and she never saw them again. It's for sure that Pap did not care for Mom's parents, especially her dad.

As Pap opened the barn door, he remembered that he hadn't started the tractor for a few days. If the battery was dead, Mr. Probus would have a real problem. Fortunately, with a little choke and a puff of ether on the air filter, the Massey Harris-50 fired right up. Bud watched out the kitchen window as the tractor's headlights came on. Pap always kept a log chain snaked through the front bumper of the tractor so he didn't have to dig around the shop looking for it. Pap drove the tractor up through the deep snow to the house and stopped in the driveway beside the woodshed.

Mr. Probus finished his coffee and waded through the snow across the backyard. He climbed onto the tractor with Pap and sat down on one of the fenders as they headed out for the creek. As they plowed through a snowdrift in the corner of the drive, the snow was almost halfway up the back tractor tires. The front tires were completely covered as they pushed through the drifting snow. Bud thought about all that wasted work he and his brothers had done the day before shoveling out a path to the Salt River Road. He was glad he brought home the sugar earlier that day instead of the next. As he peered out the front window at the blowing snow, Mom was in the kitchen making a fresh pot of coffee and praying out loud.

"Lord, please help Pap and Mr. Probus make it down to the creek safely. Help them get that car pulled out of the snowdrift. Help Mr. Probus and his poor wife make it to the hospital before that baby comes. And help Pap make it back home safe to a warm house and a hot cup of coffee."

As Pap and Mr. Probus drove through the blowing snow and down the hill to the creek, Pap was already trying to figure out how he was going to pull that car out of the snowdrift. The road dropped down between two banks just before it crossed the creek. Snow had drifted between those two banks, and the car was stuck in the snow, all the way up to the hood. Pap reckoned he would have to pull the car out backward. He could then use the tractor to wallow down a path through the drift. Finally, he could hook onto the front of the car, pull it all the way through the creek, and up the other side. He could hear Mrs. Probus inside the car, cold and moaning in the pains of labor. Pap turned the tractor around and backed up to the trunk of the car. It was a '49 Ford sedan, heavy as a tank.

"See if you can get under the car enough to hook the chain around the rear axle," Pap instructed Mr. Probus as he unwound the log chain from the front bumper of the tractor.

"No, I can't even see the axle! It is completed packed with snow under the car. Just let me hook it to the rear bumper brackets. If it pulls the bumper off the car, we will just be without a bumper. We have to get this car pulled out, one way or another!"

Thankfully, the bumper brackets were strong, and Pap was able to pull the car backward out of the snowdrift and up to a wide spot in the road. Then he drove the tractor off the road and around the car to wallow out a path through the snowdrift, through the creek, and up the other side. Pap backed the tractor up to the front of the car. Mr. Probus rehitched the chain to a front bumper bracket. Pap revved up the engine on the tractor, and Mr. Probus revved up the engine in the Ford. Mrs. Probus prayed. Off they went, plowing through the snow, through the creek, and all the way up the hill on the other side. Pap didn't stop until they reached the intersection at the Tar Hill store. There, they unhooked the chain from the car, and Mr. Probus sped off toward the Grayson County Hospital in Leitchfield.

Pap had been gone for several hours. Mom and the boys were all starting to get worried. Finally, Bud heard the tractor coming down the lane. He ran to the living room window in time to watch the tractor's headlights pierce the darkness as Pap popped over the hill. Pap parked the tractor in the barn and made his way up to the house.

"Did you get there in time?" Mom asked.

"Yeah, we got them pulled out and on their way to the hospital. I tell you they were in a bad spot. I cannot believe that man walked all the way to our house to get help. It must be two miles, and in snow that deep! He is a lucky man, and she is a lucky woman."

"Here, Pap, have a cup of hot coffee to warm your bones. And get out of those clothes before you catch pneumonia."

While Pap thawed out and warmed up by the stove, he and Mom stayed up to talk some more and sip coffee. It was too late for them to go back to sleep. But Bud was too tired to stay awake any longer. Even though the sun would be coming up in a few hours, he needed some sleep. Besides, tomorrow was going to be an all-day sled riding day! Bud curled up under the bed sheets and quilts and dozed off to sleep.

Lights Out

Even before the crack of dawn, Bud and his brothers were awake and out of bed. Mom had their hot oatmeal ready. The boys gobbled up their oatmeal and got bundled in a hurry. Winter coats, extra pairs of socks, insulated gloves, knit toboggans, and five-buckle boots. This was the first big snowfall of the year, and the boys were excited about trying out their new sled. Their old sleds were wooden, with two-by-four wooden runners. They rubbed the runners down with beeswax to help the sleds run faster, but they were still slow. Last summer, Pap had built them a new sled with steel runners made from buggy springs. It promised to be a lot faster, and the boys couldn't wait to try it out!

But first, they had to tamp down a sledding path through the deep snow on the hillside behind the chicken house. So up and down the hill they went, stomping one foot beside the other. It was tedious, exhaustive work and took up most of the morning. The boys decided to go back to the house, thaw out a bit, eat some lunch, and then have all afternoon to sled ride.

Pap had other plans. "Boys, after lunch we need to load up some wood and take it down to the Dennis family. They are almost out of firewood, and the weather is too bad to cut any now."

"What? How can they be out of firewood already?"

Bud remembered cutting wood with the Dennis boys last fall. There were six Dennis boys in all. The oldest was about Jimbo's age, and the rest were stair-stepped down, about a year apart. Between the two families, there were lots of hands available for gathering firewood. One load cut, split, and stacked for them. And a load for us. Back and forth until both woodsheds were full. How could they be out of firewood when Bud's woodshed was still half full?

Pap already had the mules hitched to the sled and was waiting by the woodshed while the boys ate lunch. Once they were bundled up again, Jimbo, Hank, and Bud helped Pap load down the sled with firewood from their own woodshed.

"OK, that looks like a couple of ricks of wood on the sled. That should do it. Let's go, boys!"

Jake and Gus were big, strong mules about eighteen hands tall. They had no trouble pulling the sled load of wood through the snow. Pap walked behind the sled, holding the reins, and the boys trekked behind. There wasn't any traffic on the Salt River Road so they made good time. As they rounded the corner and approached the Dennis house, Bud spotted a problem right away. Smoke was pouring from the chimney and the front door was standing wide open! Mr. Dennis and several of his boys were standing outside the front door, waiting.

Pap stopped the mules next to the Dennis family woodshed. He told Hank and Jimbo to unload the sled and stack the wood under the shed, which was just about empty. The bigger Dennis boys ran to help. Pap and Bud went inside the house with Mr. Dennis. The cob burner stove in the living room was white hot.

"Mr. Dennis, why is your front door standing wide open, in the middle of this bad weather?"

"Well," Mr. Dennis started to explain, "the wind was howling and blowing snow in around the windows, and we had to board them up. Now we have to leave the door open to let light into the house."

Bud's jaw dropped open. *These people ain't real bright,* he thought. *No wonder they're out of wood already.* Pap must have read Bud's mind because he took one look at Bud's face and sent him outside to help his brothers unload the sled. As he was going out the open door, Bud heard Pap tell Mr. Dennis that we would be back as soon as the weather cleared and fix the windows.

By time all the wood was unloaded and stacked, and they got back home, it was suppertime. Too late for any sled riding today!

Next morning, the boys were up and out the door early before Pap had another job for them. They grabbed the sleds, which were leaning up against the yard fence, and headed around the chicken house. Hank declared that he would be the first to try the new sled, so Jimbo and Bud pulled their old wooden sleds to the top of the hill. Holding their sleds to their chests, the boys ran downhill until they began to lose their balance and then belly flopped down on their sleds headfirst. To steer, they would simply drop the toe of one boot or the other into the snow behind the sled. At first, the new sled with the steel runners didn't perform very well. Its runner blades were thinner and tended to cut through the layers of loose snow instead of floating on top. Hank argued it would get faster as the hillside snow packed down and turned to ice. He was right. With each run, the sleds made it farther and farther down the hill. Soon they were sliding under the barbed wire fence at the bottom of hill and into the stream on the other side.

Having conquered this slope, the boys decided to try a different hill. Behind the corncrib, there was a steeper hill with a path about six feet wide running between two parallel gullies. The only problem was a black oak tree in the middle of the sled path, about halfway down the hill. The boys reckoned that they would have to go between the tree and the gully, on one side or the other. To avoid running into a gully, or hitting the tree head-on, whoever was on the sled had better be able to steer!

One by one, the boys took turns on the old sleds, packing down the snow. Soon it was time to try the new sled. Of course, Hank had to be the first one down the hill on it. As Bud watched Hank head down, it was obvious to him that this sled was *much* faster than the other two. He wasn't even sure he wanted to try it, at least not on this hill.

After watching Hank and Jimbo make several more runs, and paying close attention to their steering, Bud worked up the nerve to try it himself. Down the hill he went! Right away, Bud knew he was in trouble. No matter how hard he tried, the sled would not turn. Wouldn't turn right. Wouldn't turn left. He could see the black oak tree approaching, but instead of rolling off the side of the sled, he tried frantically to get it to turn. *Wham!* Bud hit the tree head-on. He saw a flash of light and felt a sharp pain in his head and neck, and that was it. Lights out!

When Bud finally came to, he was lying on the new sled at the top of the hill by the corncrib. Hank and Jimbo were dragging him to the house, thinking he was dead for sure. Bud's head and neck were throbbing when the boys got up to the house. Mom gave him some aspirin and made him a cup of hot tea. Even though it was still early in the day, Mom let them know that sled riding was over for the day. She told Jimbo and Hank to keep an eye on Bud and not let him go to sleep. They were not too happy about that. Not only were they missing the rest of the day sled riding, but now they had to babysit their little brother who couldn't even steer a sled.

Mom's Christmas Tree

Mom could tell the boys were disappointed about being stuck inside the house. She sent Jimbo and Hank outside to get a bowl of fresh snow for snow cream. With cream and sugar added, it tasted like a milk shake, with more ice. Mom popped the boys some popcorn and suggested they spend the rest of the day putting together a jigsaw puzzle. Jimbo dug through the toy box and found a puzzle of a winter mountain scene with a lake in the foreground and snow-covered peaks in the background. They spread out the pieces on the kitchen table and started sorting them. All the straight edges in one pile for the border, and the others separated by color.

After she finished washing and drying the dishes, Mom sat down at the table and helped the boys with the puzzle. Before long, the boys focused on the challenge of the jigsaw puzzle and forgot about playing in the snow.

Mom said the snowstorm reminded her of her childhood and of snows at Christmastime. How she and her sister helped grandpa find a suitable pine tree to cut down for a

Christmas tree. How she and her sister used a needle and thread to make popcorn garland for the tree. Bud could tell those were happy memories for Mom. It sounded like fun!

"Why don't we ever have a Christmas tree?" Bud wondered out loud.

"Oh no, Pap would never allow that! And do not tell him we even discussed it!"

"Why would Pap get so bent out of shape over a Christmas tree, or Christmas at all for that matter?" Bud asked.

Mom explained that Pap was convinced that Christ was not born at Christmas but in the springtime. Something about Mary going to visit her cousin Elizabeth during the sixth month of the Jewish calendar and staying for three months. Pap said that anybody could do the math and know that Christ was born in the springtime, same as the baby lambs in the Christmas story. Pap declared that December 25 was a pagan Roman holiday of some kind, and his family would have no part of it. Bud wondered why Pap was the only one who felt that way. Could everyone else but Pap be wrong about Christmas?

Bud decided that one day in the spring, when it warmed up, he and Mom would climb to the top of the hill behind the barn. Bud remembered a little cedar tree there and they could decorate it with popcorn garland. They wouldn't let Pap know. Then he would dig up that little cedar tree and plant it in the corner of the yard. Mom could look out the kitchen window and see a Christmas tree anytime she liked.

It would be their secret. And maybe he would work up the nerve to ask Pap about Christmas again.

Bud stayed inside the house for the next three days. He missed out on a lot of sled riding, waiting for his headaches and stiff neck to clear up. Jimbo and Hank stayed outside most of the time, riding sleds on every hillside on the farm. Bud read books, worked on jigsaw puzzles, and helped Mom around the house. One day, Mom made her special recipe jam cake and let Bud lick the bowl all by himself. He felt good that his brothers didn't even know what they were missing.

Jimbo and Hank were tired to the bone when they finally came in for the evening. No sooner than they finished supper, they were snuggled under the quilts, sound asleep.

Frozen, Stiff as a Board

"Pap, get up! Something is wrong! Dusty keeps running to the top of the hill behind the barn, then back to the house. He will not stop barking. He senses something is wrong over that hill. You and the boys need to go see what is going on!"

Mom peered anxiously out the back kitchen window, in the direction of the corncrib. It was barely daylight outside as Pap and the boys got bundled up and headed out into the cold, crisp, morning air. Dusty, their cocker spaniel, was going crazy, barking frantically, and struggling to run back and forth in the snow.

As they stopped at the top of the hill and looked down at the valley below, Bud spotted trouble right away.

"Look! There's somebody sitting under that big cedar tree, at the bottom of the hill, on this side of the fence. See? By the creek!"

Pap had a bad feeling about all this. He recognized Knobby Auberry's hat and yelled out at Knobby. No answer. No movement. As they waded through the snowdrifts and approached the creek, it was clear that Knobby was dead under that big, old cedar tree. Frozen to death in the middle of the night. Bud could see where Knobby had crossed the creek, struggling to climb up the bank on this side. Knobby had slipped and fallen several times in the deep snow and must have been exhausted from the effort. It appeared he was worn out and decided to rest for a bit under the tree.

The cedar limbs were flocked with snow, but it was dry underneath the branches. Knobby was sitting with his back up against the tree trunk. He was wearing a new pair of Duck Bill overalls and a red, plaid flannel shirt underneath his winter coat. A bottle of Old Forrester was still clutched in his right hand, not quite empty. And a redbird sat chirping on a limb just above his head.

Knobby had stopped by Bud's house just a few days ago and warmed up by the wood stove. The snow hadn't started yet, but Mom had heard the forecast on the radio. It was calling for heavy snow on top of cold weather. Knobby said he was on his way over to Ed Risinger's house about two miles away. Mom knew he was probably going over there to get drunk. She warned him to stay home, but Knobby went anyway. Apparently, he and Ed Risinger started drinking before the snowfall. After a two-day bender, he must have taken a shortcut across Raymond Crandall's farm on the way home.

Bud had never seen anyone dead before, except at Rogers's Funeral Home in Clarkson. He just stood and stared at Knobby Auberry, frozen stiff as a board under that cedar tree. Bud wondered if Knobby Auberry even knew he was dead, or if he was feeling anything.

"Bud, climb back up that hill and go over to the Hisers' house. Have them call Ben Rogers to come get Knobby's dead body. Jimbo, you and Hank go hitch the mules up to the sled and bring them back down here. Oh, and get some ropes. We'll have to lay Knobby on his side and tie him down to the sled."

Mom and Pap did not have a phone. They used to have a wall phone with a crank magneto on the right side. When the crank was turned, it charged up the battery, but it also caused all the neighbors' phones to ring. All the neighbors were hooked up to the same phone line. So each house had a distinctive ring pattern. Two long rings, followed by a short. A long, a short, and another long. When the phone rang, Mom or Pap would listen to the ring pattern to see if the call was for them. Unfortunately, lightning struck the phone line and burned out the magnetos, destroying the phone system in Limp, Kentucky.

The Hiser family owned a dairy farm and had plenty of money, so they hooked up to the new public phone system. Pap didn't want another bill to pay, so Mom and Pap did not have a phone anymore. They used the Hisers' phone in case of an emergency. This was definitely an emergency. Bud stopped by the house to let Mom know about Knobby Auberry and to warm up a bit. As he headed over to the Hisers, he kept thinking about Knobby. He wondered how Ben Rogers would get Knobby straightened out enough to get him into a casket. Maybe if Mr. Rogers propped

Knobby up by the stove, his body would thaw out enough to straighten. Or maybe Ben Rogers would have to break his legs to get him in a casket. Bud imagined Knobby showing up in front of St. Peter at the Pearly Gates drunk, with two broken legs. Right then at that moment, Bud decided he did not want to be an undertaker when he grew up.

Or a drunk.

Tobacco Bed

The cold weather seemed like it would stick around forever. Bud and his brothers spent the whole next week playing out in the snow. Riding sleds, making snow cream, building snowmen, climbing in and out of the igloo, and not thinking once about school. As it turned out, it was almost a month before the winter storm broke. Finally, the temperature warmed up and the roads were clear enough for school to resume. By then, Bud was tired of snow and ready to get back to school. Bud was ready for spring! Surely enough, springtime did arrive. And springtime brought new chores to the farm.

"Come on, boys. We need to start cutting brush and clearing out fencerows to burn the tobacco bed."

Pap had already been down at the barn, sharpening all the axes. He hitched up the mules to the sled and the tractor to the wagon. Hank drove the mule team, and Pap drove the tractor. For days, they cut brush from thickets and fencerows and piled it high onto the wagon and sled. Then Pap and the boys stacked brush crosswise of the tobacco bed, ten feet wide and a hundred feet long. It was a huge pile of brush, waiting to be torched.

After letting the brush pile dry out for a few weeks, Pap poured kerosene on the pile and set it afire. And boy, what a fire it was! Flames leaped thirty feet into the sky, along the full length of the plant bed. It burned all day and into the night. Surely, no weed or grass seeds could have survived that inferno. After a few days of cooling off, the boys raked the plant bed to remove any remaining embers or unburned limbs. Then they cut long, straight, poplar poles, about six inches in diameter, to run along the outside edges of the bed. These would be used to nail down the canvas. They placed quart Mason jars upside down in the midline of the plant bed, to hold the canvas off the ground.

Pap had already mixed the tobacco seeds himself. Tobacco seeds are so tiny you can barely see them. Pap mixed the seeds with cornmeal and broadcast them by hand, inside the poles. Another light raking to cover the seeds, and it was time to install the canvas. Tobacco canvas resembles gauze mesh, but finer. It is designed to let air, water, and light into the plant bed, while keeping out bugs or any other critters that would like to eat the tender tobacco plants as they sprouted.

Bud helped Hank stretch out the canvas over the bed. Pap and Jimbo drove nails through the metal eyelets into the border poles. When they were done, the canvas was as tight as a banjo head. Pap planted turnip seeds along the outsides of the border poles. When it came time to pull tobacco plants, they could have ripe turnips for snacks.

Good News/Bad News

When the plant bed was finished, Pap and the boys headed back to the house for lunch. Bud lagged behind as he stopped to play with Dusty. Mom called out to Bud from the back steps of the house.

"Bud, come on in the house. I have some good news for you!"

Bud was not sure what was going on, but he knew it must be something important. The whole family was sitting around the kitchen table, but there was no food on the table. Bud sat down at his end of the table, opposite Pap.

"What is going on, Mom?"

"Well, Bud, you are going to have a baby sister!"

"What? A baby sister? What good is a baby sister?"

Bud was upset and disappointed. He would not mind having a little brother, but a baby sister? What good was that? And now he would not be the youngest anymore. Bud decided right then and there that he needed to find a new place to live. Mom and the rest of the family sat around the kitchen table talking about the new girl on the way, but Bud did not hear a word. He was going to run away from home. All he could think about was making plans for his new life with a new family.

Bud trudged down to the barn and found a sturdy cane pole, with some fishing line and a hook. Bud reckoned he would need to catch some fish to eat along the way. Next, he found one of Pap's red handkerchiefs. He would wait until the kitchen was clear and fill the kerchief with some fried chicken and biscuits. Maybe he would go to Yule Howard's house and join that family. They always had plenty to eat whenever he was over there. Or maybe the Hiser family could use another son. Maybe Mr. Hodge would take him in.

Bud walked to the top of the hill behind the barn and sat down on a stack of fence posts to ponder his future. As he stared out over the valley, through his tears he noticed the big cedar tree where Knobby Auberry had frozen to death not that long ago. Bud recalled Knobby's body leaning up against the tree trunk, stiff as a board. May he'd better find a different route.

Just then, Bud heard the distinct screech of a chicken hawk circling high overhead. Lying back on the post pile and squinting up into the sky, Bud spotted the chicken hawk. He wondered what the chicken hawk was searching for. Sitting up, he noticed a group of hens digging in the dirt, searching for worms. In an instant, the hawk swooped down and latched his talons into the back of one of the smaller hens. The hen was too heavy for the hawk to gain altitude, but the hawk was able to lift the hen off the ground enough to glide to the bottom of the hill. There, amid a flurry of feathers, the chicken hawk killed and ate the hen as Bud watched helplessly.

Bud forgot about running away from home and ran back to the house. He was out of breath when he burst through the back door. "Mom, I have some bad news!"

Bud proceeded to tell Mom all about the chicken hawk and the lost hen. She told Bud she had a hard time believing his story. So he took her to the top of the hill, by the pile of posts, and let her see the pile of feathers for herself. The chicken hawk was still there, eating Mom's hen.

Mayapples and Mumblety-Peg

The next morning, Yule Howard pulled in the driveway and parked his Edsel beside Pap's Studebaker. Bud wondered if Yule had come to get Bud and take him home to the Howard family. But it turned out that Yule was just asking Pap if it was OK to hunt for ginseng on the farm. Ginseng roots are used as medicine to treat all sorts of ailments. The shape of the root indicates which part of the body it helps. Ginseng is a peculiar plant and requires a specific type of soil, good drainage, and sunlight. Ginseng is worth a lot of money. In fact, the right patch could be worth a couple of hundred dollars. Bud asked Yule how to find 'seng. Apparently, it is hard to spot. You've got to know what to look for and where to find it. So Bud asked Yule Howard if there were any other roots that were worth money that were easier to find.

"Mayapples are easy to find, and their roots are worth something. You can sell them at Risner's Hardware Store, over in Big Clifty."

Bud could not wait to tell his brothers. They were going

to be rich! Jimbo, Hank, and Bud got some empty burlap feed sacks and spades and headed over the hill to start digging their fortunes. The redbuds and dogwoods were in bloom all along the edges of the woods. The weather was warm, and the sun was shining brightly. The bottom fields were covered with mayapples. The mayapples looked like palm trees about a foot tall. Some of them had fruit about the size of a walnut that resembled a small apple. Since the fruit developed in the month of May, they were called mayapples. But the apples were of no interest to the boys. They were after the roots. Over the next few days, they filled dozens of feed sacks with mayapple roots. Hundreds and hundreds of pounds!

"But you cannot sell them like that," Pap cautioned the boys. "They have to be dried out first. Spread them out on the roof of the barn and leave them for a few days to dry in the sun."

The boys leaned a ladder up against the barn roof and spent all the next day spreading out mayapple roots until the barn roof was completely covered. After three days, they climbed back up on the roof and bagged all the roots. But an odd thing happened during those three days. The roots lost all their weight! Each bag of dried mayapple roots weighed about the same as an empty bag. After the boys sold their treasure to Riser's Hardware for about $10, they decided they needed a new way to get rich.

Pap had other ideas. "While you boys are looking for something to do, I've got a job for you. With the weather warming up, it is time to think about planting the garden. We need to clean out the barn and spread the manure on the garden plot for fertilizer. Mr. Hiser let me borrow his manure spreader, and I have plenty of pitchforks!"

The boys buckled up their five-buckle rubber boots and headed down to the barn. Cleaning cow manure out of a barn was a nasty job, no two ways about it. Pap backed the manure spreader inside the barn door, and the boys began to fill it. Different layers of the manure had different textures, different colors, and different odors. All of them were nasty. Eventually the manure spreader was piled high. Pap towed it behind the Massey Harris-50 up to the garden spot. He kicked in the power takeoff and drove around the garden while slinging cow manure high overhead. It took four loads, but finally the barn was clean. And the boys were not. They took baths beneath the waterfall in the creek to get rid of the stink. The water was ice cold, and the boys were shivering as they climbed up the rocks to get dressed. But at least they smelled better.

The next morning when Bud awoke, Pap already had the plows hooked up to the tractor and was pulling through the garden gate. Bud jumped out of bed, got dressed, and ate breakfast in a rush. Didn't even take time to put his shoes on! Plowing the garden meant it was time to go fishing! And what easier way to dig fishing worms than to just follow the plow? Bud grabbed an empty coffee can and ran to the garden just as Pap finished the first furrow. Bud followed the plow and felt the warm dirt squish up between his toes. Every now and then, Bud would spot an earthworm wiggling in the furrow, and he would pull it out of the dirt. Before

Pap finished plowing the garden, Bud had a coffee can full of fishing worms.

By then, Hank and Jimbo were up and coming out the back door. When they saw the coffee can full of worms, they got excited too! Bud washed off his feet under the faucet of the hand pump at the water well and ran inside the house to put on socks and shoes.

"Mom, we are going fishing in the creek!" Jimbo yelled through the back door as he raced down the steps.

Waving to Pap on the tractor, the boys ran down to the barn to find some fishing line, hooks, and bobbers. And a five-gallon bucket to hold their catch. Then it was off to the creek! A nice patch of cane pole bamboo was growing in the creek bottom, and there was a deep fishing hole nearby. Jimbo used his Case pocketknife to cut down three long straight cane poles, and Hank rigged up the fishing gear. They spent all morning cane pole fishing off the creek bank, pulling blue gills and crappies until the bucket was half full. Time to head back to the house and clean the fish before lunch. But before they left, Bud asked Jimbo to cut him another cane pole. Bud wanted Jimbo to show him how to make a cane pole whistle.

Mom was pleased to see the boys' catch and announced they would have fried fish for supper. They set about cleaning the fish. Mom put them in a pot of salt water to soak. After lunch, the boys went outside to make cane pole whistles. Jimbo showed Bud how to cut the cane pole just above each joint, how to smooth up the ends, and how to cut a notched opening into one side of the cane about an inch from the open end. Then Jimbo used his Case to whittle a locust stick to fit tightly into the open end of the cane. He flattened off one side of the stick just a bit and forced it into the cane. Cutting off the of the stick blush with the end of the cane was the last step in completing the whistle.

"Can I borrow your knife, Jimbo? I want to make one myself, now that you showed me how!"

"Sure, Bud, be my guest."

Bud made several cane pole whistles that day. He discovered he could adjust the pitch of the whistle by changing the size and shape of the notch or by changing the spacing between the flattened stick and the hollow cane. When he grew tired of making whistles, Bud returned the Case to Jimbo. Jimbo and Hank used the knife to play a game of mumblety-peg. Bud watched intently as his brothers took turns flipping the pocketknife off their forefingers, their elbows, and their shoulders. They scored points by getting the blades to stick in the dirt in a certain pattern. First, just the big blade, then the big and little blades together, then just the blade on the back end of the knife. Bud was fascinated. He needed a pocketknife of his own so he could practice mumblety-peg, too. But he didn't want a heavy Case pocketknife. No, Bud wanted something more his size. He remembered the three-bladed Barlow in the case at Mr. Hodge's store. Now he just needed a way to make some money to pay for it.

Pop Bottles and Claire Marie

After Lunch, Bud rode his bike up to Hodge's Store. Bud had a silver twenty-inch buzz bike with a yellow banana seat, high handlebars, and a wire basket in front. Pap had built it out of spare bike parts that he had picked out of the junk pile behind the Western Auto store in Leitchfield. Pap built bikes for Jimbo and Hank, too. Thirty-six-inch bikes with ten speeds that would go thirty miles per hour. Faster downhill! But those bikes were too tall for Bud to ride. His legs could barely reach the pedals. Bud reckoned the buzz bike was just the right size for him.

Bud pushed through the screen door of Hodge's Store.

Mr. Hodge was sweeping the floor with his one good arm. "Hi, Bud! How can I help you today?"

"Well, Mr. Hodge, I need to make some money. I want to save up to buy that three-bladed Barlow pocketknife in your showcase there."

"Tell you what, Bud. I've got some ideas for you. I need someone to help me wash my truck, and someone to mow my yard. It is hard doing all that with just one arm. I will be happy to hire you for that. And here is another idea. Why don't you use that bike of yours to collect glass soda bottles along the road? A lot of people just throw them out the car window when they are done, and those bottles are worth money. You can bring them into the store, and I will pay you a penny for each one."

Bud was thrilled at the chance to make some money. He ran out the screen door and jumped off the front porch of the store, onto his bike, and was off in a hurry pedaling down the Salt River Road in search of pop bottles. Sure enough, right away he spotted a Nehi Grape bottle, and then a Royal Crown Cola. By the time he reached the intersection with Highway 347, the wire basket on the front of his bike was half full of Coca-Cola, Pepsi-Cola, Orange Crush, and even a Chocolate Yoo-Hoo bottles. On the way back to Hodge's Store, he finished filling the basket. He couldn't wait to turn in his bottles and collect some change!

"Eighteen bottles, Bud! That is eighteen cents!"

"How much is the three-bladed Barlow?"

"Two dollars."

"Wow! I will have that saved up in no time!"

"Come back tomorrow and help me wash the truck, and I will pay you a dollar."

"OK, Mr. Hodge! See you in the morning!"

As Bud rode back to his house, he was so excited the wheels of the buzz bike were barely touching the ground. Bud had trouble sleeping that night. He kept thinking about helping wash Mr. Hodge's truck the next morning and earning more money for that pocketknife. He popped out of bed at daylight and wolfed down his oatmeal as soon as it was cool enough to swallow.

Mr. Hodge had just opened the store when Bud pushed through the screen door.

"I'm here to help wash your truck, Mr. Hodge! When do we start?"

"Tell you what, Bud. Why don't you go round up some more pop bottles? We can wash the truck after lunch."

"OK. I'll be back in a couple of hours. I'm going to ride around the blacktop road toward Big Clifty and see what I can find."

Riding out the Salt River Road, Bud found a couple of more bottles tossed in the ditch just since yesterday and saved them in the basket. At the end of the road, across from Gilbert Hay's house, he turned right onto Highway 347. It was smooth riding. Bud decided he liked riding on blacktop a lot better than on the gravel Salt River Road. He kept one eye on the road and one eye on the ditch as he pedaled along watching for pop bottles. Whenever he spotted one, he stopped and added it to the collection.

Around the curve at Wilbur Cook's house. Past the old Moore Schoolhouse. Up the lane that led back to Clyde Hay's house across from Junior Franklin's place. Down the long stretch toward Wallace Crawford's house and the Moore Cemetery. As he neared the curve in front of Ed Risinger's lane, Bud thought about Knobby Auberry and wondered if Ed Risinger was sober this morning. Or drunk already. Pete Cain was loading his D6 dozer on the lowboy trailer, and Bud stopped to watch. Mr. Cain was a big man, strong as an ox, but he looked small up on that dozer. As Pete Cain eased the Cat up the ramps, the front half stood up and then slowly settled onto the trailer bed. He made it look easy, and Bud was fascinated. But he was on a mission in search of pop bottles, so Bud pedaled on down the road.

And then he spotted it! Another buzz bike! It was off in the distance riding in circles on the blacktop road in front of Fred Powell's house. Bud did not remember any kids living in that house so he pedaled on down the road to see who it was. As he got closer, Bud realized the kid on the bike was a girl about his age. She was wearing white shorts and a baby-blue shirt with pink tennis shoes. She had long, brown hair, parted in the middle, with a bit of a cowlick. With a round face and squinty eyes, she reminded Bud of a baby squirrel or a rabbit.

"Hi. My name is Bud. Do you live here? In Fred Powell's house?"

"Yes. I'm Claire Marie. My mom and dad bought this house, and we just moved in. Mom is going to be the fifth grade teacher at Western Elementary, and Dad is the principal. Paula and Bill Edmonds."

"Cool. I love school, and your mom is going to be my teacher, I guess."

"Then I will be in your class. Why do you have all those empty pop bottles in your basket?"

Bud explained about saving money to buy that new three-bladed Barlow pocketknife and how to play mumblety-peg. Claire Marie did not seem to understand anything Bud was talking about. So Claire Marie and Bud just rode circles together in the highway.

Bud lost track of time, for some reason. A woman's voice calling out the side door of Fred Powell's house interrupted their fun.

"Claire Marie! Come in the house! It is time for lunch!"

Bud suddenly remembered he needed to get back and help Mr. Hodge wash the truck. He said goodbye to his new friend and started pedaling back toward Limp. But he stopped for a moment and looked back over his shoulder long enough to watch Claire Marie park her bike under the big maple tree in the front yard. As she headed around the corner of the house, Bud saw her look over her shoulder. At him. Bud felt a little dizzy and had trouble keeping his bike out of the ditch. He completely forgot to look for bottles. Bud's stomach started to growl. Mom always had lunch ready at 12:00 noon, and Bud always ate lunch at 12:00 noon. Bud looked up at the sun and realized it was around one o'clock. No wonder he wasn't feeling well. It didn't have anything to do with Claire Marie, surely.

Bud unloaded his pop bottles onto Mr. Hodge's countertop. Twenty-eight of them. That meant twenty-eight cents. Added to the eighteen cents from yesterday, Bud had already saved forty-six cents. A dollar for helping wash the truck, and Bud would have over half the money for that Barlow. But first, he had to eat!

"Mr. Hodge, can I go home and eat lunch before we start on that truck?"

"Sure, Bud. Go on home and eat. We will see you after a while."

Bud rode home as fast as he could and ate some brown beans and cornbread. His lunch was a little cold since Bud has missed his lunchtime. But he didn't mind. At least it stopped the growling in his stomach.

Looking Sharp

Before long, he was back at Mr. Hodge's store, ready to go to work. Mr. Hodge had already pulled the Dodge pickup under a big maple shade tree in the front yard. He spotted Bud riding up on his bike. Mr. Hodge waved at Bud with his left arm.

"Here, Bud, climb up on the roof of the truck and give it a good scrubbing. Then climb down and get the hood. I can't reach them."

Bud peeked at Mr. Hodge's stump of a right arm but did not ask any questions. He reckoned Mr. Hodge needed some help and was willing to pay. That was enough for Bud. Besides, he liked hanging out with Mr. Hodge. He remembered riding to Leitchfield with Mr. Hodge once. Bud marveled at how Mr. Hodge shifted gears. The Dodge had a three-speed manual transmission, with the gear shift on the steering column. Mr. Hodge would push his right stump up against the steering wheel and reach across with his left arm to shift gears. It looked a little dangerous, but he seemed to have the hang of it. The Dodge did not have any dents.

Bud climbed up in the bed of the pickup and then onto the roof. Mr. Hodge handed him a bucket of soapy water and a sponge. Bud gave the top of the cab a good scrubbing, and Mr. Hodge handed him the garden hose to rinse it off. Bud worked his way from the top down, washing the hood, the windows, then the doors and fenders, and finally the front grill and back tailgate. When it was all rinsed off, that Dodge shined like it was brand new! Bud was proud of his work, and even prouder of the dollar bill Mr. Hodge gave him. Fifty-four more pop bottles, and that Barlow pocketknife would be his!

When Bud got back home, he noticed that Pap had run the disk over the garden plot several times. Mom reminded Bud and his brothers not to make any plans for tomorrow. It was time to plant the garden. The garden plot, which sat directly behind the house, had been a junk pile when Mom and Pap bought the place. Occasionally, they would dig up a stray nut, a bolt, or a strange hunk of metal. But it was really good black dirt. They always grew a good garden there.

Next morning, the boys tied tobacco sticks to the ends of long strings of baling twine. They staked off the garden rows four feet apart. They used hoes to build a mound down half of one row, for the carrots, lettuce, and radishes. Four rows of tomato plants. One row of bell peppers. Four rows of sweet corn. Four rows of bunch beans. Two rows of pole beans. Six rows of potatoes. A row of sweet potatoes, and a row of peanuts. Finally, in the lower half of the garden, they hilled up round mounds for the cantaloupes, cucumbers, watermelons, and yellow squash.

Altogether, the garden was almost half an acre. It was surrounded by an eight-foot, woven-wire fence to keep the chickens and wild animals out. Growing a garden of this size meant a lot of work hoeing and weeding, but it also provided Bud and his family with plenty of fresh food. Every year, Mom filled the far room of the house with enough canned fruit and vegetables to last through the winter.

With weather warming up, Pap decided the boys needed haircuts. Pap had an old barber's chair down in the shop. It was red with chrome trim pieces. It had a hydraulic pump in the base with a foot pedal for raising and lowering the seat. Pap served as the neighborhood barber, at least for the men of the Limp community. Most of them would stop by once a month to "get their ears lowered" while they caught up on the latest news. Pap cut the boys' hair too, but those haircuts were quicker and more straightforward. They got burr haircuts. Pap just removed the head from the electric clippers and with a few strokes was finished.

Jimbo, being older, needed to look sharp for the girls. He persuaded Pap to let him wear a flattop. Pap had a special comb with long teeth he used as a platform for the clippers. Flatten the top and cut it short on the sides and around the back. At least it had a little style, not like a burr haircut. When Jimbo added a dab or two of Brylcreem and combed it just right, that flattop looked good. But Bud always ended up with a burr, which he did not like. At all.

"Your turn, Bud! What kind of cut would you like today?"

"Short around the ears and in back. And leave it a little long on top so I can have a part."

Pap always gave Hank a good haircut, long enough he could part his hair on one side. Stylish enough to look presentable. Bud had a double crown, and the hair between those crowns liked to stick straight up. He was convinced that his hair would lie down, just like Hank's, if Pap would just leave it long enough. But he knew that wouldn't happen. It was always the same thing.

"OK, Bud, I'm done. Here look in the mirror. How do you like it?"

"Looks great, Pap! Thank you!"

"Oh, wait a minute. I left it a little long in the back. Oops! I slipped and there is a gap in the back. Do you want me to leave it? Or try to smooth it out so it's not so noticeable?"

"Go ahead and take out the gap"

Bud's family did not have a TV, so he had never seen a show called *The Little Rascals.* But he did know who Alfalfa was. The kids at school mad fun of Bud, calling him Alfalfa because his hair stuck up, too. A burr was the only haircut Bud ever remembered having. He just hoped Claire Marie would not make fun of him.

Striped Bass

Next Morning when Bud rolled out of bed, Jimbo and Hand were already removing the canvas from the tobacco bed. Time to pull weeds and grass from the plant bed. Bud hated this chore. It was tedious pulling the weeds and grass while not disturbing the tender tobacco plants. Pap laid long boards across the log poles so the boys would not have to step in the plant bed to get to the middle.

After an hour or so of trying to stay balanced on one of those boards, it was all Bud could do to stand up straight. He decided he would rather kneel outside the logs and pull weeds around the edges. Jimbo and Hank would pull the weeds in the center of the bed. Either way, it was tedious work and Bud didn't care for it. By the time the bed was clean, and the canvas stretched again, it was time for lunch.

Mom had warmed up the pinto beans and cornbread left over from supper and made a beef pot roast. They didn't eat meat very often because it was too expensive. Bud's eyes lit up when he saw the pot roast in the center of the table. Pap sat at one end of the table and Bud at the other. Jimbo and

Hank sat on a bench on the side of the table next to back kitchen windows. Mom sat across from them. One seat was empty. Bud guessed it would be for his new baby sister. He reckoned his seat would be next to her. He reckoned he did not like that idea.

When they had cleaned their plates, Mom announced a surprise for dessert. Mom went into the far room and returned with a cherry pie that she had cooked while everyone was out of the house. Then she went to the freezer and pulled out a tray of homemade vanilla ice cream! Wow! Mom fixed each one a bowl of cherry pie with ice cream on top, and the boys gobbled it up. Hank found a seed in his pie, like always. If you had ten gallons of canned cherries and there was only one seed in all of it, Hank would be sure to get that seed. He just had a knack for it.

Saturday was a day of rest for Bud's family. Adhering to the Mosaic law of the Old Testament, Pap allowed no work from sunset Friday to sunset Saturday. No work, period. But fishing was OK.

"How would you boys like to go fishing with me? I am going down to Hardin Springs to fish below the dam at the old grist mill. I hear the fish are running upstream and getting stuck in the pool below the dam."

The boys jumped at the chance for some easy fishing, and they all piled into the Studebaker. When they drove down the hill to Hardin Springs, Pap stopped at Bill Gray's store to fill the minnow buckets and ask how the fishing had been. Bill Gray and Pap were cousins, on their mom's side of the family. Bill Gray's store was not as big as Hodge's store, but it had the same Colonial Bread push bar on the screen door. Mr. Gray sold bait, since he was right in the middle of Hardin Springs and just up the road from Rough Creek. He told Pap that this morning he had already seen several stringers full of striped bass—nice-sized ones too!

Apparently, news about the good fishing had gotten around the whole community because there was no place to park close to Rough Creek. Pap had to just pull off into the grass alongside Highway 84 and hope no one ran into the car. They grabbed all the fishing fear from the trunk of the Studebaker and headed toward the dam.

Sure enough, the banks were lined with fishermen. Bud could see bobbers popping up and down as some people fished with floats. Others cast artificial baits into the creek and reeled them back in. Shiny silver spoons, purple worms, plugs, and jig baits with horsehair tails. Anything to attract the attention of one of those stripers!

Since there was no room to stand and fish along the banks, Pap and the boys climbed atop the foundation walls of the old mill. Rough Creek was spilling over the dam about six inches. The water above the dam was calm and glassy, but below the dam, the water was churning. They settled on a nice spot to fish and rigged up their rods. Hank was the first to get a line in the water. As soon as the minnow hit the water, a fish grabbed it and pulled his bobber under the water. This fish was serious about getting loose from the hook. Hank's Zebco 303 reel was squealing loudly.

Hank had to tighten the clutch on his reel because that fish was running. If Hank couldn't slow it down, his line would surely get tangled up with other lines already in the water. Hank cranked for a while and then let the fish run for a while. Finally, the fish wore down, and Hank was able to reel it in. His rod was bent to the point of breaking as he lifted his catch out of the creek. Pap snatched the fish before it could break free, using the long-handled fishing net. Pap laid it on top of the cooler, which had measurements marked on the lid. Fifteen inches long. Pap weighed it at almost three pounds.

By the time Bud got his line in the water, Hank had already caught another one. As Hank was fighting with this catch, Bud's float disappeared. The tug on his line was so sharp it almost snatched the rod and reel right out of his hands! Bud started cranking furiously. Pap yelled at Bud, coaching him to let the fish run for a little bit or he would break the line. Finally, Bud calmed down and began to work the fish like he had seen Hank do. Crank it in a little. Let it run a little. As Pap was catching Hank's second fish in the net, Bud's fish was wearing down. Pap helped Bud get the fish up to the top of the mill's foundation wall. It was twelve inches long and weighed a pound and twelve ounces.

As the day went along, people were reeling in striped bass all up and down the creek. But nobody caught as many as Hank. He spit on the hook every time before attaching the bait, and the bass must have liked the smell of his spit. Hank always had a better idea, whether it came to fishing or anything else. Pap and Jimbo caught their share as well, and by lunchtime, the stringer was full, doubled up in fact, with two fish on each snap ring. They gathered up all their fishing gear and the stringer of fish and walked up the hill to the Studebaker. Pap stopped by Bill Gray's store and proudly showed him the stringer of fish. Mr. Gray congratulated Pap and said it was as nice as any stringer he had seen all day. The boys couldn't wait to get home to show Mom!

Mom did not like cleaning fish. She didn't mind cooking them, but she would not clean fish. If you caught them, you had to clean them. That was her rule. She set up a bench outside the back door and gave the boys a roasting pan to hold the fish. Jimbo and Hank filleted the fish in no time. Mom rolled them in a batter of cornmeal and eggs and fried the fish in her favorite iron skillet. They were perfect!

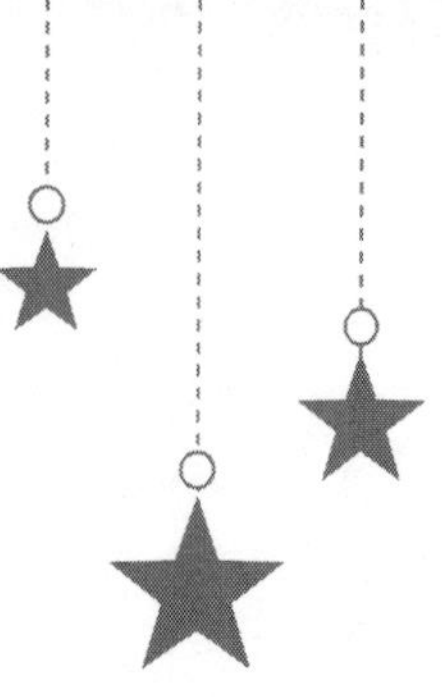

Bud's Own Barlow

Sunday morning came. Bud hopped on his buzz bike headed toward Big Clifty on Highway 347. His intent was to gather up all the pop bottles he had missed on the return trip before. And maybe, just maybe, Claire Marie would be out on her bike again! But no such luck. There wasn't even a car in the driveway. Bud was awfully disappointed but turned around and set about the task of searching for empty bottles. It was a long trip back to Mr. Hodge's store, but Bud managed to find another basketful of pop bottles and turned them in. Twenty bottles in all. That left him thirty-four bottles short of getting that Barlow pocketknife.

"You look a little down today, Bud. What is wrong?"

"Well, I was hoping to have enough bottles to get that knife today."

He did not bother to confess that he was just disappointed because Claire Marie Edmonds was not home. The fact of the matter was that Bud was a little embarrassed by that.

"You know, I still need someone to mow the yard. Maybe you can do that."

Aha! That was the answer! Bud's mood improved in a second.

Mr. Hodge went to the tool shed and got the push mower, a twenty-inch Western Auto model with a Briggs and Stratton motor. He checked the oil, gassed up the mower, and got it started. He said, "I will watch you make a few rounds until you get the hang of it."

Mowing with the push mower was not all that hard, Bud thought. At least not on the flat ground in the front yard. Mowing the hill by the front ditch was a different story. Bud had to walk in the ditch while pushing the mower sideways along the bank. Bud quickly got the hang of that too, and soon the front yard was finished. Mowing was going to be an easy way to make money! When he got around back of the house though, he began to change his mind. Mrs. Hodge had apple trees in the backyard that had to be mowed around. Mr. Hodge had the mower deck on the lowest setting. Between the mole trails and the fallen apples under the trees, Bud struggled to push the mower.

If that was not enough, there was a muddy spot up next to the house where wastewater from the kitchen sink drained into the yard. It had blue-green slime growing in it, and it stank to high heaven! Bud walked around that spot and tried to mow it without stepping in the mess. It took him a couple of hours to finish, but Mr. Hodge said it looked as neat as a pin and was happy to pay Bud his $5.

Bud wondered why he didn't just start off mowing yards in the first place.

"Can we go back over to the store now, Mr. Hodge?"

"Sure, Bud. Is there something you want to buy?" Mr. Hodge asked with a twinkle in his eye.

"Yes, sir, I've had my mind set on that Barlow pocketknife for a while now!"

As they climbed the steps and walked through the screened front door, Bud's heart was beating in his throat. He stood with both hands on the glass showcase, drumming his fingers while Mr. Hodge went behind the counter to get that knife. Bud handed Mr. Hodge two $1 bills. Mr. Hodge handed Bud the three-bladed Barlow. Bud could hardly hold his excitement! He opened each of the blades and snapped them shut. The back springs were nice and firm. He tested the blades and each one was sharp. He ran his fingertips over the side handles and the Barlow emblem. The Barlow was his! He stuck it in the right front pocket of his jeans and headed home to show Hank and Jimbo. Every so often, along the way Bud checked to make sure it had not fallen out of his pocket. Mr. Hodge stood on the front porch of the store, watching Bud and smiling.

Do It Right or Go to the House

Pap had another job waiting for Bud and his brothers. "Boys, we need to fix the fence between us and Mr. Crandall. It is down in a couple of places, and I do not want the cows getting out."

Jimbo and Hank hooked up the trailer to the Massey Harris and loaded all the fencing tools and materials. A dozen black locust posts from the pile at the top of the hill. Posthole diggers, shovels, spodge bar for tamping, rolls of barbed wire, hammers, staples, and fence stretchers. Sledgehammers and rock chisels. Pap was very particular when it came to building fences. Step, step, long step. Ten feet. Posts had to be set exactly ten feet apart, regardless. If there was a stump in the way, it had to be dug out. If there was a rock in the way, it had to be dug out or chiseled through. Bud remembered Jimbo and Hank taking turns chiseling out a posthole in solid sandstone, rather than moving the hole a foot or so either way. It took them all day to dig that one posthole.

"Do it right or go to the house!"

That was Pap's favorite saying. Rather than walk all the way back up the hill to the shop to get the sledgehammers and rock chisels, it was better just to load them now. The property line between Pap's farm and Mr. Crandall's farm ran along a creek. In a couple of places, the creek has washed out under the trees that root wadded and fell across the creek. In other places, posts had rotted and broken off at the ground. The boys knew they would have a hard day's work ahead. Pap paced off and staked the hole locations, and Hank and Jimbo set about digging holes. Luckily, they didn't run into any rock ledges. They had the posts set and tamped in a couple of hours. Bud helped Pap unroll the barbed wire and Pap stretched it tight. The boys started stapling the barbed wire to the posts. Bud wasn't big enough to dig postholes or tamp posts, but he was big enough to drive staples.

Just as Bud was about to fasten the fence to a six-inch cedar, Pap yelled at him. "Bud! What are you doing?"

"Well, I am nailing the barbed wire to this cedar tree. It is right in line, ten feet from the last post—"

"Bud, do it right or go to the house!"

Bud was confused. He did not see how he was doing anything wrong. But if Pap wanted him to go to the house, well, Bud just figured he would go to the house! So he dropped his hammer and staples and headed up the hill toward the house. When Jimbo and Hank got back to the house for supper, they were in a foul mood. When Bud left and went to the house, it just left them with more work to do. Plus, they had to spend the day with Pap. And Pap was not happy! Neither of the older boys had ever taken him up on his offer to go the house.

"Come here, Bud!" Hank grabbed Bud by the earlobe and pulled him outside. "Let me explain to you about building fences! And about Pap. See, when Pap said to do it right or go to the house, he really did not consider it an option. What he really meant was to just do it right!"

"But I don't understand what I was doing wrong. That cedar tree was in line with the fence, and it was ten feet from the last post. What did I do wrong?"

"Well, Bud, there are two types of fence posts. Line posts and corner posts. A line post doesn't do much. It just stands there and keeps the wires eight inches apart. That's it. A corner post, on the other hand, is responsible for the entire run of fence. If it fails, the whole fence will collapse. So a corner post is thicker. It is set in the ground deeper. It is braced better. Bud, when you looked at that six-inch cedar, you saw it as a line post. When Pap looked at it, he saw that someday it would grow into a corner post, which is much more valuable."

"That makes sense, I guess. But why didn't Pap explain that to me himself?"

"That's just not how Pap is. Get used to it!"

As the days got longer and the weather got hotter, Pap found lots of jobs to keep the boys busy. He sent them out into the pasture fields with grubbing hoes and axes to cut bushes. Bud preferred to use the foot adze. A foot adze resembled a heavy hoe and was used to square up logs for building the walls of log houses or log barns. Bud wasn't as big or as strong as Hank or Jimbo, but the heavy foot adze did most of the work. One chop and it would cut through almost any bush in the field. They boys kept a clear glass gallon jug of water stashed away under a shade tree and stopped to rest and drink when they overheated.

It took them a week to clear all the pastures, but it kept Bud out of Pap's hair for a week. And nobody told him to do it right or go to the house.

Next, Pap decided the boys needed to pick up all the rocks in the pastures and pile them up. After they piled up all the rocks in the pastures, Pap drove from pile to pile with the tractor and trailer to load up the rocks. Then they unloaded the rocks in the driveway and busted them into gravel, using three-pound sledgehammers. It wasn't as pretty as gravel from the rock quarry, but it was cheap enough.

Polebridge Missionary Baptist Church

Between summer chores, Bud took every opportunity to ride around Highway 347 looking for empty glass pop bottles. It was fun. It got him out of Pap's sight. And it was an easy way to make some money. But the main reason he rode around Highway 347 was to visit with Claire Marie. Her house had a front porch swing just right for carrying on conversation. Claire Marie's beagle puppy, named Jesse, sat on the swing between them. Jesse was the chaperone, and Mr. Edmonds was OK with that.

One day, Claire Marie invited Bud to go for a walk in the woods, down to the creek behind her house. It was a gorgeous, warm, sunny day in June. Bud and Claire Marie wandered along the path through the woods and came upon a huge boulder as big as a car. The sun was shining through a break in the trees and warmed the rock. Bud and Claire Marie climbed on top of the boulder and sat down in the sun. They discussed all kinds of things. Like how she got that hole in the back of her leg.

"Oh, that is from a bike wreck. The pedal tore the back of my leg and it got infected. It took a long time to heal and left that hole."

"I'll bet that hurt! A lot!"

"Yeah, but it is OK now. Mom says it's just my beauty mark."

Claire Marie's parents were older than most kids' parents, but not as old as Pap. Pap was forty-five years old when Bud was born. He was really more like a grandfather than a dad. Claire Marie said her parents didn't have any kids for so long that they just figured they could not have any. Then she came along. Her mom and dad called Claire Marie their miracle baby. Claire Marie liked talking about her mom and dad. Bud wondered if Claire Marie's mom would be a good teacher. She seemed nice enough, but you never knew.

"Bud, my mom asked me if you go to church and if you would like to go to church with us some Sunday."

Bud was feeling suddenly uncomfortable. The only times he had ever been inside a church was for funerals. Pap listened to Herbert W. Armstrong on the radio, broadcasting sermons from the Worldwide Church of God all the way from Pasadena, California. Every month, Pap sent money to California. In return, every month Pap received the latest copy of *The Plain Truth* magazine. Bud loved to read the magazine, which was filled with stories from the Old Testament. But the illustrations in those stories were frightening. Horror gripped the faces of the guilty, just before they met their doom. Bud reckoned that God was someone to be feared. So Bud feared God. But he didn't go to church.

"Uh, do you go to church, Claire Marie?"

Obviously, she did, because she had just invited him. But Bud was caught off guard, and his mind wasn't working exactly right.

"Yes, I do. We attend the Polebridge Missionary Baptist Church on the Salt River Road, over toward Howevalley. Why don't you go to church with us this Sunday?"

So that was why Claire Marie and her parents weren't home the day Bud rode by their house. It was Sunday, and they were at church.

"I don't know. I will have to ask my mom first."

Bud figured he could ask Mom, but definitely not Pap. Bud was nervous on the way home, not sure how Mom would react. But he worked up the nerve to ask. To his surprise, Mom was OK with it. She said she reckoned heaven was big enough for more than one denomination, whatever that was. Bud couldn't wait to ride back to Claire Marie's house to let her know.

The next Sunday morning, Bud was up at the crack of dawn. He washed behind his ears and ran the comb through his jet-black hair. With his burr haircut, Bud's hair just stuck straight up, but he wanted to look sharp so he combed it anyway, adding a dab of Jimbo's Brylcreem. When he saw Claire Marie's parents coming in the driveway, he was waiting by the front yard gate. He didn't give Pap the chance to ask any questions. Claire Marie opened the back car door, and he sat beside her in the back seat. It was a gorgeous day!

Polebridge Missionary Baptist Church was a little white church in the woods. It had been a one-room schoolhouse that closed when Western Elementary School was built over on Highway 84. The gravel parking lot was not big enough to hold all the cars, so Mr. Edmonds had to park in the grass under a big oak tree. They were a little late, and the singing had already started when they slipped in the back door. They found a seat at the end of a back pew. A young man in an oversized suit jacket was speaking from behind the podium. Bud kept waiting for him to shut up so the preacher could talk. But it turned out this young man *was* the preacher. Brother John R. Clark. He had his Bible open in his left hand and was waving his right hand like he was riding a wild horse.

He talked about sin. And Hell. And getting saved. Sometimes he got pretty loud. Finally, he calmed down and offered an invitation. Anyone who wanted to get saved needed to step out of their pew, come up front, and accept Jesus as their personal Savior. Bud started remembering all the sins he had already committed, sins that Brother John R. Clark had just finished talking about. Bud sure didn't want to go to Hell. The Holy Spirit got hold of him. While the church sang "Just as I Am," Bud found himself stepping out into the aisle and staring blindly at the preacher. As he slowly made his way to the front, Bud could feel people reach out from the pews and pat him on the back. Bud was scared to death. Brother John R. Clark placed his hand on Bud's shoulder.

"What is your name, young man?

"Bud. My name is Bud."

"Well, Bud, do you repent of all your sins? Do you accept Jesus Christ as our Lord and Savior?"

"Yes, I guess. Yes, sir, I do."

"Good! Church, can I hear a hallelujah? Can I get an amen?"

Bud got saved that day, before he even knew what hit him. He was quiet on the ride home, and so were Claire Marie and her parents. Bud was not sure exactly what had just happened, but he felt like he was floating on air and sick to his stomach at the same time. He needed to talk about it with Mom. But not Pap.

Arthur Ray's New Buick

The Edmonds dropped Bud off in the driveway and he ran inside to look for Mom. But she wasn't in the house, which caused him to panic.

Just then, Mom came rushing in through the back door. "What in the world is going on behind Mr. Crandall's barn?"

Bud and his brothers followed Mom back outside to see an old black car cutting doughnuts behind the barn on the next ridge. Its engine revved as it went round and round in tight circles, throwing rooster tails of dirt and rocks into the air. The boys hopped on their bikes and pedaled over to Arthur Ray Wooden's house as fast as they could go. Just as they arrived, Arthur Ray drove around the side of the barn and parked under a shade tree by his house.

"How do you like my new car? It's a '48 Buick! Two-door coupe. V-8 with three-speed on the column!"

As they were checking out Arthur Ray's new Buick, Mr. Crandall himself came ripping down the driveway in his old, green Chevy pickup truck. A thick trail of dust trailed behind him. As he sped past, Bud could tell Mr. Crandall was upset. He didn't even stop at the house. Bud and his brothers, along with Arthur Ray, ran around the side of the barn to find Mr. Crandall screaming at the top of his lungs. His face was bloodred.

"What in the world are you doing, Arthur Ray Wooden? It has taken me twenty years to get grass to grow on this ridge! And it has taken you all of twenty minutes to tear it all up!"

Arthur Ray and his mom lived in a mobile home on Mr. Crandall's farm. Mr. Crandall was Arthur Ray's grandfather. He was a tall man, a carpenter who wore carpenter's overalls with a loop on each leg to hold a framing hammer. Mr. Crandall was normally a quiet man, but Bud got to see a different side of him that day. Bud reckoned that Pap wasn't the only one who got bent out of shape sometimes. Arthur Ray left his Buick parked under that shade tree. In fact, it would stay parked there the rest of summer and into the fall. Until the grass grew back. Bud often looked across the holler to see Arthur Ray out behind the barn, walking around the ridge, checking for new shoots of grass. (Eventually, it would grow back, but not until almost time for the first frost in October.)

Aunt Matt

Bud woke up every morning that summer thinking about collecting pop bottles and mowing Mr. Hodge's yard to make money. But today he would not get to do any of that. Today was Wednesday, and that meant a grocery trip to Houchen's Market in Leitchfield and a stop to visit Aunt Matt in Clarkson. Aunt Matt was Pap's mother. Her name was really Matilda Whitworth, but everybody just called her Aunt Matt. She was the only grandparent Bud ever had. His other grandma and both his grandfathers had died before he was born. Bud really did not like Aunt Matt. She was old, cantankerous, and downright mean, and she did not have any use for kids or their energy. She lived alone in a house that Grandpa Powell left her in his will "so long as she remained his widow." If she ever remarried, the house would go to her children. So she never remarried. Not that any man would want to marry her anyway.

Grandpa Willie's first wife died during childbirth with their first child, Corbett. Grandpa married Aunt Matt because he could not raise a child by himself. Aunt Matt was only fourteen years old when they married, and she did not like the baby Corbett because he wasn't her child. One day, Grandpa came in early for lunch and caught Aunt Matt trying to smother Corbett with a pillow. Grandpa took Corbett to his brother's house and let them raise him. Maybe that was why Aunt Matt was so mean, but whatever the reason, she seemed to enjoy taking it out on Bud and his brothers.

Aunt Matt had cheese apple trees in the back corner of her place, but the boys were not allowed to eat any of them. The apples just lay on the ground to rot, or the yellow jackets ate them. She had Concord grapevines along the fence between the yard and the tobacco patch. They were loaded with grapes in late summertime, but if the boys ate any of them, they had to eat seeds and skins. Aunt Matt would walk around the yard after they left, looking for grape seeds and apple cores. If she found any, the boys were sure to get a whipping from Pap. She kept a bucket of drinking water on the kitchen counter, with a dipper. But you had to drink all the water you dipped out. No water could be poured back into the bucket. It just wasn't sanitary, she said.

Aunt Matt had rocking chairs in the living room. The boys were allowed to sit in them, but only if they kept the heels of their shoes on the floor. In other words, they were not allowed to rock in those rocking chairs. Mostly, the boys just sat in the car with the windows rolled down while Pap visited with Aunt Matt. They were always glad to see Pap finally come out of the house and get in the Studebaker so they could leave.

The route home took them past the Clarkson High School, where a baseball game was underway. Pap asked if the boys would like to stop and watch the game. Of course! Pap had been coach of a baseball team in Big Clifty when he was younger and often talked to the boys about the game of baseball. He envisioned them growing up to be shortstops. Pap was convinced the shortstop was the most critical position on the team. Pap parked the car, and they found a good spot in the grass to enjoy the game. Bud marveled at the players in their white uniforms with black numbers stitched on the back, their caps with the big block letter "C" on the front, and their new leather gloves. Maybe one day he would get to play shortstop on a baseball team. Maybe one day he could do something right and Pap would be proud of him.

The game action was exciting, from the sounds of the pitches hitting the catcher's mitt, the call of the umpire behind the plate, and the crack of the bat when someone got a hit. During the seventh-inning stretch, a couple of teenage boys carrying wooden crates of ten-ounce Coca-Cola glass bottles approached them. "Would you boys like an ice-cold Coca-Cola?"

"Sure!"

"OK, that will be a dime apiece."

Bud's heart sank into his stomach, and he could feel his face turning beet red. He did not have a dime. And neither did his brothers. The teenage boys laughed at Bud and his brothers. Bud felt the teenagers had tricked him and his brothers. He was humiliated. Bud decided that city folks could not be trusted.

He asked Pap if they could hang around after the game was over so he could pick up all the empty Coke bottles to turn in at Mr. Hodge's store. Then he would have a dime in his pocket the next time they came to Clarkson.

Setting Tobacco

Pap told the boys that they would be pulling tobacco plants the next morning and setting tobacco in the evening. Once the sun got low, the plants would not wilt and would take root overnight.

Sure enough, next morning Pap had the wagon piled up with empty burlap feed sacks. It was hitched to the tractor and waiting by the plant bed while the boys ate breakfast. One hundred plants arranged neatly, wrapped in a feed sack, tied with a grass string, and piled in the shade under the wagon. Pap had a half-acre tobacco base, so they needed twenty sacks of plants.

Every time they filled a bag, the boys took a break and pulled up a turnip for a snack. With all four of them working together, they had all the plants pulled in time for a late lunch. They loaded all the bundles on the wagon, parked it alongside the tobacco patch, and placed the plants back under the wagon until later when the sun would be lower in the sky. After lunch, Jimbo and Hank helped Pap hook up the drag-type tobacco setter to the Massey Harris-50. They drove down to the creek and filled the tank with water. By four o'clock, they were ready to set tobacco.

Pap always drove the tractor because he did not trust anyone else to drive in a straight line. Jimbo and Hank sat on either side of the setter. The setter had a metal shoe that split the soil into a narrow furrow about three inches wide. The valve at the bottom of the water tank was attached to a cog with a chain to the axle. Every two feet, the valve opened and dumped water into the furrow. Jimbo and Hank took turns sticking the roots of the tobacco plants into the furrow whenever the water dumped. Heavy metal wheels on the back of the setter then closed the furrow around the plants and packed the dirt. Bud's job was to follow the setter and uncover any plants that got run over and to keep the boys' plant trays full. Bud spent the afternoon running back and forth, carrying bundles of plants and uncovering plants. It was getting late in the day when they finished. The sun was setting when they headed back to the house. They admired the straight rows of the newly set tobacco patch.

July Birthdays

July was one of Bud's favorite times. Not because of the heat or endless hours of hoeing the garden or the tobacco patch. Nope. July was the month for birthdays! Bud and Mom were both born in July. So were several members of Yule Howard' family. In fact, Bud and Kenny Howard were born on the same day. Imagine that! Each year, Pap and Yule Howard would pick a date in July and both families would gather at the Howard farm. When the date rolled around, Bud and his family piled into the Studebaker and drove over. When they arrived, Yule's wife Bonnie was trying without success to catch some chickens to make chicken and dumplings. The Studebaker had barely rolled to a stop when Hank jumped out.

"Want me to catch those chickens for you?"

"Yes, Hank. I sure would appreciate it! I am all out of breath."

"No problem! Do you have any empty peach baskets?"

Hank was quick on his feet, and he loved a challenge. In

no time, Hank had two hens cornered against the yard fence and pinned them under the peach backets.

"Can you kill them for me, Hank? I am a little squeamish about that."

"Sure. Have you got a sharp hatchet?"

Hank grabbed one of the chickens and had Jimbo hold it down on a stump. Hank whacked off its head with one chop of the hatchet. Jimbo turned loose and that headless chicken ran round and round in circles in the backyard, flapping its wings. Then they killed the other one the same way. A couple of times the chickens ran into each other and fell over. But they always seemed to get back on their feet and start running again. Bud reckoned they couldn't see where they were going, being headless and all. Bonnie Howard had a washtub filled with scalding hot water ready on the back porch. When the chickens stopped flopping, Hank dunked them in the water to loosen the feathers. Then the boys took turns plucking all the feathers from those dead chickens.

"Good job, boys! Roberta and I can take it from here!"

Mom and Bonnie sat around the tub cutting up the chickens, and the boys went off to play. Yule had slung a rope over a big limb of the oak shade tree in the side yard. His sons Eddie and Stan showed Bud and his brothers how to swing on it and do all kinds of tricks. They swung all the way around the tree. They swung upside down. They played mumblety-peg with their pocketknives, and Bud got to show off his new Barlow. After Bud won a few games of mumblety-peg, the older boys decided they would rather ride bikes up and down the gravel road out front.

The men sat in rocking chairs on the back porch, listening to country music on the radio. George Jones, Merle Haggard, and Marty Robbins. They chewed tobacco and spit the juice into an empty coffee can. Yule chewed Red Man, but Pap preferred Apple brand plug chewing tobacco. He said it was sweeter than the Red Man twist. Yule's dad, Willie Howard, leaned against the back of the house, in a cane-bottom, straight-back chair, and told one story after another. Pap and Willie fished together once or twice a week. Between them, they shared enough stories to write a book.

Willie swore there was a catfish in the creek behind his house that was too big to turn around. It had one red eye and one green eye, so the other fish would know which side to pass on. Willie was determined to catch this catfish. He fashioned a hook out of the point of a double shovel plow and attached it to the end of a hundred-foot log chain. He hooked the other end of the chain to the drag disc parked at the end of the potato patch by the creek. When that catfish swallowed the hook, it lit out up the creek faster than Willie could run and pulled that disc all the way through the potato patch before it broke the chain. And Willie was left with a patch of French fries. Willie had emphysema and wheezed a lot, especially when he got excited. Wheezing, coughing, and slapping his legs, Willie barely finished his tale when the women announced it was time to eat.

Mom hollered out the front door for the boys to come

into the house. They lined up around the kitchen table and piled their plates high with a feast fit for a king. Chicken and dumplings, sliced red tomatoes, green beans, mashed potatoes, cornbread, and homemade biscuits. Mom made her special jam cake for dessert. It was really a birthday cake, although it did not have any candles. Pap would not agree to that.

After supper, they all relaxed and just visited. Finally, Mom reminded Pap that they needed to get home so she could milk the cows. So they all piled back into the Studebaker. As they drove past Fred Powell's house, Bud peeked out the side window to catch a glimpse of Claire Marie playing with her beagle pup in the front yard. What an exciting day!

Baptism Sunday

As summer went along, Bud found himself spending more and more time at Claire Marie's house. Sometimes they played in the creek behind her house. It didn't have a lot of water running in it, just the trickle of a wet-weather stream. One day, Bud borrowed a hammer and chisel from Mr. Edmond's tool shed and carved hearts in a huge flat rock in the creek bed. Probably still there to this day. Most Sundays, Bud rode to church with Claire Marie and her family. He gradually began to learn some of the most popular church hymns, at least enough to sing along. And he learned that Brother John R. Clark wasn't really a young teenager after all. He just looked like it. When John R. preached, Bud found himself paying close attention. He preached in a style different from Herbert W. Armstrong on the radio, and in a different tone. Not as polished. More down to earth. But louder—definitely louder. Effective, too. Almost a dozen people came forward and got saved over the summer. Bud was thrilled when one day, Claire Marie stepped out and got saved herself!

Brother John R. Clark announced one Sunday that the church was going to schedule a baptism in two weeks, now that the water in Linder's Creek was warm enough. Being a converted one-room schoolhouse, the Polebridge Missionary Church did not have a baptistry. All their baptisms were performed in Linder's Creek, but only when the water was warm. On Baptism Sunday, Bud didn't ride to church with Claire Marie's family. Instead, he had Mom make him an early breakfast. As the sun was coming up, Bud rode his buzz bike along the Salt River Road to the new bridge over Linder's Creek. He laid the bike in the ditch and walked up the bank to sit on a pier under the bridge.

The Gideons had been to Western Elementary School earlier in the spring, passing out little New Testaments. Bud got a red one. At the time, it did not mean much to him so he took it home and put in his dresser drawer, under his T-shirts. One Sunday, John R. Clark asked everyone in church to hold up their Bibles. Bud was embarrassed because he didn't have a Bible. Then he remembered that little red New Testament and started taking it to church every Sunday. On Baptism Sunday, Bud tucked it into his back pocket, in case he had to answer any questions at his baptism. He had never been to a baptism and did not know what to expect. As he sat under the bridge, Bud read the onion skin pages of the little red book. He made it all the way through the book of Matthew before the crowd started to arrive.

As the congregation stood on a gravel bar beside a bend in the creek, everyone who was scheduled to be baptized put on white robes. Brother John R. Clark put on a white robe too and waded into the creek, about waist-deep. Then one by one the newly saved waded out to him. He allowed each one to cover their nose and mouth with their right hand. Then he baptized them by dipping them backward until they were completely underwater and then raising them up again.

Suddenly it was Bud's turn. The water was not as warm as Bud had expected. It was more like ice water, and Bud began to shiver. He wondered if maybe they should have postponed the baptisms for another month. He took a deep breath, placed his right hand over his mouth, and pinched his nose.

"Bud, because of your faith in Jesus Christ as your personal Lord and Savior, I now baptize you in the name of the Father, and the Son, and the Holy Spirit!"

And under Bud went!

When he popped back up out of the water, Bud was freezing cold and shaking all over. He could not wait to get back on the gravel bar. He slipped on a rock, lost his footing, and went down to his knees. Bud realized that he almost got baptized twice in the same day! Fortunately, Brother John R. Clark's wife, Gladys, was waiting with a warm towel to dry off and wrap up in.

Bud thawed out and dried out just in time to watch Claire Marie get baptized. She handled it a lot better than Bud and emerged from the water with a huge grin on her face and her arms lifted high in victory. Bud felt guilty that he had not been that excited about his own baptism. Still, it was a good feeling. A *really* good feeling. Like a huge weight had been lifted off his shoulders. And now that he was dried out and warmed up again, Bud noticed that the sun was shining through the trees onto the gravel bar where the church was gathered.

After everyone was baptized, Brother Clark had a brief sermon, and Gladys led the church in a rousing rendition of "Amazing Grace." And it was over.

Gradually, folks made their way back to their cars and left. Bud walked with Claire Marie to her car, and they said their goodbyes. Bud did not even worry that his hair was a mess. It was a long ride home from Linder's Creek, but Bud was in no hurry. He found himself listening to the sounds of nature and enjoying the beauty of the world along the way.

Suddenly, Bud realized that God loved him. God loved him! Bud had always feared God, but now he knew that God loved him! The tires of the buzz bike floated along the blacktop pavement. Even when he hit the graveled section of the Salt River Road to his house, it was as smooth as glass. He couldn't wipe the grin off his face as he parked his bike by the woodshed.

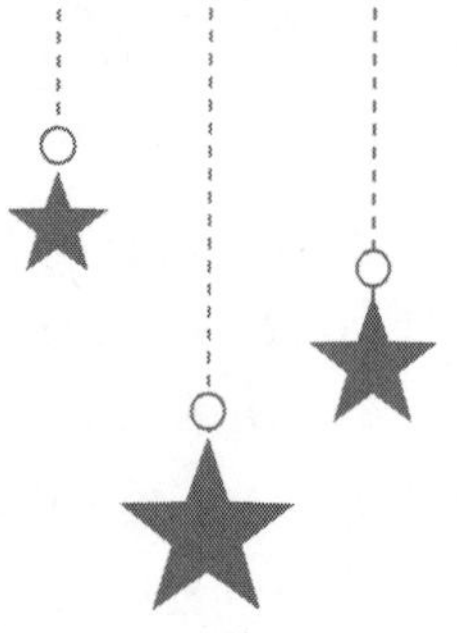

Big Six Henderson

"**What is all** the commotion in the front field?" Mom asked nobody in particular.

Mom was gazing out the side kitchen window, straining to see Pap and a strange man having an animated discussion in the hayfield across from the Hisers' driveway. At first, she thought it might be Pap arguing with the next-door neighbor about the property line. Pap claimed Mr. Miller had dug up the corner survey rock and moved it about ten feet to steal some of Pap's farm. Yes, the property line had a bend in it, at the edge of the woods. Pap thought it should be a straight line. That's what the deed said.

Maybe Jimbo and Hank needed to go check on Pap before things got out of hand. About that time, she noticed the two men coming toward the house. She and the boys went outside to meet them in the front yard and see what was going on. The stranger was tall and had a .45 revolver in a leather holster on his belt. He wore a brown jacket with a silver badge on the left pocket.

"This man is Big Six Henderson," Pap explained. "He is a revenuer and wants to camp out overnight on the back of our farm. He thinks the Portman boys are making moonshine down in the holler by the creek. He wants to be there first thing in the morning when they fire up the still."

Mr. Henderson walked back out to the Salt River Road to get his car and parked in front of the Studebaker, beside the woodshed. He didn't want anyone to spot his car. It was getting late so Mom invited Big Six Henderson to join the family for supper. Big Six said he would like to hang out at the house until dark and then make his way down to the holler. Bud's house didn't have air conditioning, just a window fan to stir the hot, sticky air. Bud and his family often sat outside while watching the stars or chasing lightning bugs until the house cooled down. So they went outside after supper.

They all sat in a circle in lawn chairs while Big Six entertained them with stories from his adventures as a revenuer. Bud especially enjoyed one tale about how they busted a huge moonshine operation up a holler in the mountains of eastern Kentucky. The revenuers had known about these moonshiners for years but had never been able to bust the operation. The local sheriff was on their payroll and tipped them off anytime the revenuers came around. So Big Six and his agents had to slip into town unannounced. There was only one road into and out of that holler. As Big Six and the other revenuers headed down that road, they came to a cabin. A little boy about Bud's age was swinging on the front porch.

"Where is your dad, son?" Big Six Henderson asked the boy.

"He's at work."

"Where is he working?"

"Can't tell you."

"Look, I will give you a $20 bill if you tell me where your dad is working."

"Fine, give it to me now."

"I will give it to you when we get back."

"Mister, you best give it to me now!" said the little boy as he looked up at Big Six Henderson, "because you ain't coming back!"

Big Six gave the boy $20 and followed his directions down the road. Big Six said they had an awful shootout back in the holler. The moonshiners had lookouts with deer rifles on top of the hills overlooking the road. When they finally spotted the revenue agents coming up the road, they opened fire. But eventually Big Six and his boys fought their way through the barrage of bullets. They busted up dozens of barrels full of moonshine, arrested the moonshiners, and took the copper condensation coils for evidence.

"Jimbo, I need you and Hank to go down to the barn and fill up two five-gallon buckets of dry cow manure for Mr. Henderson. He uses it to fertilize his tomato plants."

Big Six Henderson raised tomatoes for the Kentucky State Fair competition every year. He reckoned some of Pap's cow manure would be just the secret to winning another blue ribbon. Bud looked back over his shoulder as they walked back to the barn and saw Big Six Henderson hand Pap a $20 bill. Price of admission, he reckoned. Bud told his brothers what he had seen. As the boys shoveled the buckets full of cow manure, Hank decided to play a trick on Big Six. After he left to go to the woods, Hank found a couple of wide watermelon rinds in the chicken yard. Jimbo jacked up the back of the car, and Hank placed a watermelon rind under each of the back tires. They let the jack back down. They could not wait to see what happened when Big Six tried to leave.

Before the sun even came up, they were awakened by the sound of Big Six revving his engine like he was in a hurry to go somewhere. For some reason, the car wouldn't move. The boys just lay in bed and laughed. Finally, the rear tires burned through the watermelon rinds and gained some traction. Big Six tore out up the driveway, slinging gravel the whole time. He swerved to avoid hitting the Studebaker and cut through the tobacco patch, knocking over plants along the way. Never even stopped. Pap was sure to be bent out of shape over the tobacco patch getting torn up. It was a good thing Willie Howard had already picked up Pap before the crack of dawn to go fishing. The boys ran to hide the watermelon rinds behind the chicken house and never let on to Pap what really happened.

"The price of cow manure just went up," Hank figured. "Twenty dollars a bucket next time!"

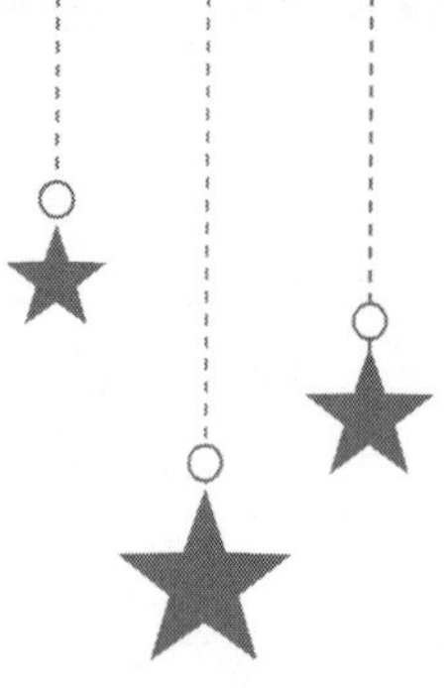

Powell Family Reunion

The first Sunday in August was approaching, and it was time for the Powell family reunion. Bud loved the reunion! It was a time to see all his cousins from the city and listen to stories from all his aunts and uncles. And they had some whoppers to tell. Lloyd and Gladys were always the first to arrive. Gladys was a really nice lady, very proper. Her brother was the county school superintendent, and her family included educated people. Lloyd was Pap's cousin. He was just an old country boy who moved to Elizabethtown and made good for himself. He owned several businesses and lived in a stone house high up on a hill. Each year for the reunion, Lloyd brought his favorite straight-back chair for his own personal use. He loved to rock that chair back on its back legs while telling stories. One year he busted the woven cane bottom right out of it, in the middle of one of his tall tales. He re-caned it with strips of rubber inner tubes so now when he got excited, the seat would bounce up and down.

Uncle Chester was always in charge of making the coffee. He brought his own coffeepot and set it up just outside the living room window. Uncle Chester was a firefighter at Ft. Knox so he knew a thing or two about making coffee. He made it black and strong. Bud reckoned firefighters needed strong coffee. Anybody who did not like it black and strong could add milk, cream, or sugar—or all three.

One of Bud's favorites was Uncle Walter Finch, who was married to Pap's sister Norma. All the boys anxiously awaited his arrival. Uncle Walter always drove a Buick, and he always had a trunk full of iced-down, ten-ounce glass bottles of Coca-Cola. Again this year, Uncle Walter did not disappoint. Man, what a treat! When Uncle Walter popped the metal tops off those glass bottles, the soda gushed out. Bud tried to drink it quickly before it lost its fizz. Uncle Walter got the biggest kick out of watching the boys enjoy those Coca-Colas.

Pap pulled the wagon under the shade tree by the driveway, and Mom and Aunt Nervie covered it with tablecloths. Aunt Nervie was Lloyd's mother. She was about the same age as Aunt Matt but had a completely different personality. Aunt Nervie was a great cook. Her specialty was something called mincemeat pie. Bud was not sure exactly what was in a mincemeat pie except raisins, but it sure was good! Bud secretly wondered why Aunt Nervie couldn't have been his grandma instead of Aunt Matt. As each car or truck arrived, the women sorted out the food. Meats on this side of the wagon. Side dishes over here. Cakes and desserts down there. Mom's hand-squeezed lemonade, jugs of tea, and other drinks on the end of the wagon. The entire wagon was covered with food. Pap asked his cousin Pete Finch to ask the blessing, and everyone joined in reciting the Lord's Prayer.

Bud and the other boys usually held a contest to see who could eat the most. One plate, two plates, another plate of cakes and pies. A watermelon seed-spitting contest to top it all off! Man, what a day! Bud's stomach was so full he felt like a tick ready to burst. He found an empty chair close to Lloyd Powell to hear some of his tall tales. After their food had settled, all the cousins chose up sides and had a softball game in the front field, where the ground was flat. The cousins from Louisville played on real teams, so they were good. Bud's team got beat, but he had a great time anyway. But Hank got a little upset over losing the ball game. He had a bright idea to get back at his cousins.

Hank convinced his cousins that he could hold onto the electric fence without getting shocked. They didn't realize he was standing in a spot where he could watch the light on the electric fence box and follow its timing. When the light went off, Hank would grab the fence. When it was time for the light to come back on, he would turn loose. One by one, all the city cousins tried it, and they all got shocked. This fence box was a bush burner, so it carried a punch and several of the cousins got knocked to their knees from the shock. These city kids were not so bright after all.

Some of Bud's cousins picked up corncobs from around the crib and chicken feathers from the chicken yard. They inserted two or three of the feathers into one end of the corncobs and tossed them through the air like missiles. Mom didn't mind the city kids playing in the chicken yard, but she got upset when they started chasing the chickens. She said those hens would stop laying eggs for a week and they needed the eggs! So the kids decided to play tag in the tier poles of the tobacco barn. Bud marveled at the things that entertained his cousins from the city. But most of all, it was great just getting together to play with all his cousins. He was sad to think it would not happen again until next year.

The tobacco crop was looking good with the leaves lapping in the middle of the rows by reunion day. Pap was proud to show it off to all the men there, as they shared memories of tobacco patches from their own childhoods.

Top, Sucker, and Prime

By the end of August, the tobacco plants were as tall as Jimbo, and blooming. Pap declared it was time to top and sucker the crop. Bud was not tall enough to top the tobacco, but he was tall enough to sucker the plants. Jimbo and Hank walked through the patch row by row, breaking out the top of each tobacco stalk while Bud and Pap followed, snapping out the suckers that sprouted out between the leaves and the stalk. The blooms and the suckers pulled energy from the leaves and would hurt the crop. Pap removed the suckers with each hand so he could sucker two rows at a time. Bud was happy to sucker one row at a time because he could keep up that way. Back and forth they worked until the whole patch was topped and suckered.

After the patch was topped and suckered, it still had to be suckered a couple of more times as new suckers developed. And the patch had to be primed as the plants ripened. Basically, the boys had to get up at sunrise, before the dew lifted, and crawl through the patch while snapping off the lower leaves from each stalk. Those leaves were already starting to dry up and would just crumble to dust if they were left on the stalks. But crawling through the patch in the morning dew meant getting wet and muddy. Bud learned to watch the blooms on the morning glory vines that grew in the tobacco patch. If the blooms were open, the dew was still on. Once the blooms closed up, the dew was lifted and they had to stop, to avoid crumbling the leaves. When they were finished, bundles of trash leaves tied with rubber bands lay scattered throughout the patch. The boys got up early again the next morning to crawl through the patch, gathering up all the bundles of trash leaves. They placed the bundles of leaves on tobacco sticks and hung them in the barn to finish curing. Bud hated priming tobacco. It was a messy job.

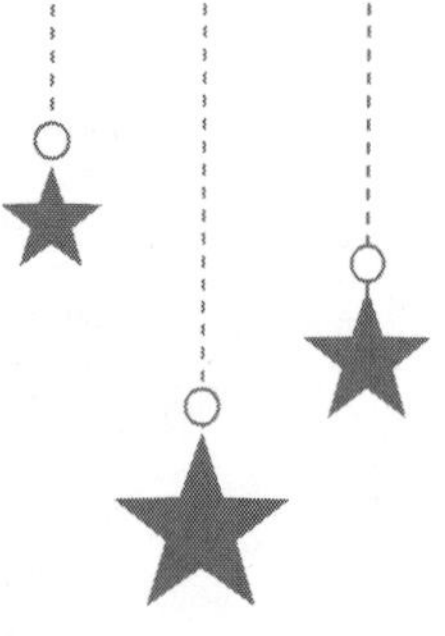

Hank's Bright Idea

Pap declared it was time to cut hay and fill the barn loft for winter. Pap used the tractor and sickle to cut the hay. After the hay lay drying in the sun for three days, Pap and the boys used two old, horse-drawn, high-wheel rakes to rake the hay into windrows and then into piles scattered throughout the hay field. Jimbo pulled one rake with the tractor, and Hank operated the rake from a metal seat high atop the rake. Pap pulled the other rake with the mules, and Bud operated that rake, using a long, levered arm to raise and lower the teeth as needed.

Jimbo said the tractor was not running right, like one cylinder was missing. Maybe it had a loose spark plug wire. Pap checked the plugs and the wires. They all seemed fine, but the Massey still did not sound right. Pap told Jimbo to unhitch his rake and pull the tractor into the shop. Pap would work on it later. They finished raking the hay with the mules. When the hay was all piled up, Pap took the mules back to the barn, unhitched the rake, and hitched up the hay wagon with its tall sideboards designed to hold loose hay.

Pap sent the boys back out to the hayfield with the mules and hay wagon to bring in the hay while he worked on the tractor.

Jake and Gus were good mules, but they did not care for the heat. They preferred to stay in the shade of the barn or at least under a shade tree. Those mules were already acting up as Jimbo drove them out to the hay field and stopped by the first haystack. Each of the boys had a long-handled pitchfork that they used to load the loose hay onto the wagon. One by one, they cleaned up the haystacks until the wagon was almost full. One more stack, and they would be ready to head to the barn.

That's when Hank noticed the spreadhead snake under the last haystack. He tried to get the snake to leave the shade of the haystack, but it wasn't cooperating. So the boys took turns jabbing at the snake with their pitchforks. The spreadhead just raised its head and spread its neck out like a cobra, hissing and sticking out its tongue. Finally, Hank stabbed the snake with his pitchfork and tossed it out into the open field. The boys finished loading the wagon. Jimbo snapped the reins. Jake and Gus just stood there. Stubborn mules! Jimbo snapped the reins across the mules' rear ends. Nothing. Now what were the boys going to do? Those mules had decided they were not going to budge, whether the wagon was empty or full. They were not going to move. Then Hank had a bright idea.

"Give me a couple pitchforks of hay off that wagon! Now Jimbo, let me borrow your Zippo lighter. We will light a fire under those stubborn mules, and I bet they will move then!"

So they did just that, building a fire under each mule. And they moved all right, just enough until the fire was no longer under them. Instead, the fire was under the wagonload of hay. It wasn't long before the whole load was on fire—the hay and the wagon! Naturally, the mules panicked and did what mules and horses always do when they are panicked by fire. They headed straight back to the safety of their barn stalls, with the boys running behind as fast as they could go. Pap saw them coming, but there was nothing he could do to head off the mules and keep them out of the barn. The mules tore the single tree hitch completely off the hay wagon as they ran through the stall door, leaving the burning load of hay directly under the hay loft. In a matter of minutes, the barn was on fire!

Pap and the boys ran back and forth from the well pump, carrying buckets of water to douse the flames, but they were fighting a losing battle. It was too far gone. Pap yelled at the boys to get all the machinery and equipment out of the barn, and they rushed to do it. Fortunately, the milk cows were still out to pasture and hadn't come to the barn for their evening milking. Bud raced to the house as fast as he could go, not knowing exactly what to do. Mom was standing in the backyard, tugging at the strings of her tattered apron with one hand and rubbing the other hand over her stomach, which was swollen with the baby sister inside. She put one hand around Bud's shoulder. Together, they just stood there in the backyard and watched the flames melt a hole through the metal barn roof above the hay loft. Soon the flames were roaring high into the air.

"Zip, zip, zip! Zing!"

The flames were so intense the heat was melting the metal roofing and molten metal tears were dripping off the edge. In a couple of hours, nothing remained of the barn but a pile of smoldering rubble and metal teardrops. Jake and Gus did not make it out.

"What in the world are we going to do? What in the world are we going to do?" Mom kept repeating the question.

Somehow, Bud knew that Mom was not talking to him. She was asking God.

Barn Raising

Over the next several days, lots of people came over to see the damage. Many of them were neighbors. Many were complete strangers. Bud was sick to his stomach as all those people stopped by to watch his family wallow in misery. But Bud was mistaken about their intent.

The next morning, Mom looked out the side kitchen window to see a caravan of trucks, tractors, and men with chains and chainsaws coming in the driveway.

"Who in the world are all these people?" Mom wondered out loud.

Pap went out to greet them in the driveway. There was Yule Howard with his son Eddie. Gilbert Hay with his sons Billy and Terry. Carlos Quiggins and Boyd Powell. Pete Cain and his boys. Mr. Crandall and Arthur Ray. Wilbur Cook and Junior Franklin. Even Mr. Probus came to help, and a dozen or more men that Bud's mom didn't even recognize. Apparently, Yule Howard had gone around the neighborhood, explaining the situation and rounding up an army of volunteers to build a new barn. Everyone he asked came through and brought others with them.

"Perci, we have come to cut some logs to take to the sawmill, to cut enough lumber to build a new barn," Yule Howard stated as he stood with his hand on Pap's shoulder. "When I was back in the woods looking for ginseng this spring, I noticed you have a lot of nice white oaks and poplars back there. I believe fifty logs will do it."

Pap, Jimbo, and Hank led the men back to the woods, and they began marking trees. Bud stayed at the house out of harm's way. Logging was dangerous work and no place for a boy Bud's age.

Later that morning, several of the neighborhood women came over with food and helped Mom prepare lunch for the men.

All day, Bud could hear the roar of chainsaws and the crash of falling trees. Bud watched from the yard fence as tractors pulled dozens of logs up out of the woods and staged them in the flat pasture field beside the workshop. Other men with cant hooks rolled the logs onto log trucks and hauled them to the sawmill. One man they called Tiny was so big and strong that he just rolled the logs onto his truck by hand. It was a steady stream of activity on the farm, organized and running as smooth as a beehive.

By suppertime, everyone was gone. Bud peeked out the living room window as Mom and Pap hugged each other under the locust tree and cried.

For the next two weeks, Pap and the boys were busy digging and pouring concrete footers and piers for the interior posts. Yule Howard came over and laid concrete block foundations for the new barn walls. When the weekend arrived, those trucks came down the driveway again. This time they were loaded with freshly cut lumber, sawhorses, Skill saws, handsaws, squares, levels, and buckets of nails. It took about an hour to get organized. What to do first? Who to do what?

Once the worksite was set up and everyone was assigned a task, they jumped right into framing the new barn. Bud and the other boys were responsible for gathering up scrap lumber to keep the job site clear of debris. And for being gofers running to get whatever materials the men needed. A string level. A framing square. More nails. Whatever the men needed.

One crew framed the outside wall for one side of the barn. Another crew assembled the opposite side. Third and fourth crews took care of the front and back walls of the barn. Finally, another group of men set the inside posts and braced everything together. Once all the walls and interior posts were set, the men started building the rafters and roof decking. By the end of the second day, the barn was framed and ready for metal roofing and siding.

The third morning, the trucks returned with metal siding and roofing as well as extension ladders. One crew stayed on the ground and handed up metal roofing, sheet by sheet, to the men atop one side of the barn. Another crew worked on the other side of the barn. They installed the roofing by using special nails with rubber washers to seal the holes and prevent leaks. Once the roof was on and the ridge cap was installed, they started on the sides of the barn. The barn doors were hung from tracks with rollers so the barn doors rolled open and shut without having to swing on hinges. A couple of guys even climbed up on the roof and installed wind turbines so the barn wouldn't build up too much heat in summer.

By the end of the week, the barn was completed and all the men gathered up their tools and went home. Mom and Pap never knew who many of those men were, where they came from, or how they heard about their barn fire. And they figured they would never see most of them again, at least not this side of heaven.

A Weekend in Eastview

Summer was drawing to a close and it was time to get ready to go back to school. Bud had been saving up his money all summer after gathering pop bottles, mowing Mr. Hodge's yard, and washing his Dodge. He had a little over $50. Bud had an eye on a three-speed Western Flyer with a speedometer at the Western Auto store in Leitchfield. Bud asked Pap if he could use his own money to buy it. That seemed fair to Pap so he drove Bud to town to pick it up. It was a beautiful bike with metallic yellow paint and a black, leather seat. It was a thirty-inch bike, but Bud had grown over the summer and could reach the pedals if he stood up. Bud couldn't wait to try it out! It was much faster than his old twenty-inch buzz bike. Bud was afraid to go too fast on the graveled Salt River Road, but Highway 347 was blacktopped and smooth. Bud got the bike up to thirty-two miles per hour in third gear and had to brake to go around the corner at Wilbur Cook's house. The sign for the curve said, "Speed Limit 25." Bud realized he was breaking the speed limit. He rode all day and was still not worn out when he came home for supper.

"Wake up, Bud! It's the first day of school!"

Mom did not have to call twice. Bud bounced out of bed and got dressed in his new school clothes. He joined his brothers at the breakfast table. They wolfed down their oatmeal and walked out the lane to catch the school bus. It had been an exciting summer and Bud could not wait to get back to school to swap stories with all his friends at Western Elementary. Bud was starting fifth grade with a new a teacher and a new principal plus a new friend named Claire Marie! Best of all, he and Claire Marie would be riding the same bus. Unless of course she rode with her mom and dad. Bud's heart dropped into his stomach when that thought crossed his mind. When Bud climbed the steps to board the bus, he noticed Claire Marie in the front seat.

"Hi, Bud! I saved you a seat!"

Now Bud was *really* excited about going back to school!

When the bus unloaded in the circle driveway at Western Elementary, it did not take Bud long to catch up with his best friend, George Miller, and swap stories about their summers. When Bud told George about his new bike, George suggested that Bud ride up to his house this weekend. Bud thought that was a great idea! They had the rest of the week to make plans for the weekend.

When school dismissed on Friday, Bud promised George that as soon as he got off the bus, he would ride his bike up to East View. When the bus dropped Bud off at the end of the lane, he ran to the house and grabbed a quick bite. Bud jumped on the Western Flyer and headed out on the ten-mile trip to East View. He was so excited he forgot to even tell Mom goodbye or where he was going for the weekend.

The ride down Crosier Hill was quite a thrill. Bud had never ridden down that hill before and didn't realize how steep it was. Bud looked at the speedometer to discover he was already up to forty miles per hour and not even halfway down the hill. Bud was a little scared because he had never been on a bike going that fast. He rode the brakes a little to reduce his speed the rest of the way to the bridge. The trip up the other side was a lot slower. Bud had to zigzag back and forth in low gear just to avoid having to stop and push. Finally, he topped the hill and had an easy ride up to Vertrees's store at the intersection with Highway 84, which went the rest of the way to East View.

Bud pedaled past Western Elementary School. It was odd that no one was there. No cars in the parking lot. No school buses. Bud had never seen the school abandoned like that, and it felt a little odd. He stopped at the top of Claggett Hill to check it out before heading over the hill. It was steeper than Crosier Hill, but Bud was feeling more confident. He decided to lay off the brakes this time. When he hit the bottom of the hill, the speedometer showed fifty miles per hour. Bud was halfway up the other side before he had to start pedaling.

In ten more minutes, he was knocking on George Miller's front door. The ten-mile trip had taken him less than thirty minutes.

Mrs. Miller seemed a little surprised to see Bud. George

forgot to say anything to his mom either. Anyway, Bud joined them for supper and the boys went outside to play. George Miller's house sat on Main Street in East View, a block from the Illinois Central railroad tracks. That block was open space so they played in that field until they heard a train coming. George asked Bud for a penny and placed it on the rail. After the train passed, that penny was flattened out so Bud could barely tell it had even been a penny. By the time the next train came through, they had gathered a bucket of cheese apples and tried throwing them through the doors of the empty box cars. It was a lot harder than Bud expected. They had to throw the apple well in front of the open doors and let the train run into it. But after several attempts, Bud was throwing apples into open boxcars almost every time. He hoped there weren't any hobos in those boxcars, or they might get an apple upside the head.

As it got close to dusk, George asked his mom if he and Bud could spend the night in the log cabin across the street from their house, next to the railroad tracks. She said it was OK so they grabbed a couple of sleeping bags, some snacks, and a flashlight and prepared to camp out for the night in the log cabin. Soon it was dark, and the boys were fast asleep.

Bud was jarred from his slumber by the rumbling of the earth and the rattling of the log cabin. A train was coming! Bud listened intently as the train got closer. He could hear it, and he could feel it as it came through the Big Clifty crossing miles away. Whistle blasts from the engine let Bud know each time the train approached a road crossing.

The rumbling and the rattling got louder. Bud shined the flashlight on George, who was sound asleep and snoring.

The log cabin was rattling violently now, and Bud had to assure himself that the log cabin was located beside the railroad tracks and not in the middle of the tracks. He wished he had told his mom that he was going to spend the weekend at George Miller's house. And he prayed! Finally, the train was right on top of them, and rushed past the cabin with such force the wind blew through the open window. Bud let out a deep breath, which he had been holding in for who knows how long now? He decided that they would find somewhere else to sleep tomorrow night!

George finally woke up, not realizing how close they had come to not seeing the sunrise. They were hungry and ready for breakfast so they walked across Main Street and in the front door of the house.

"George! What is that smell?"

"I don't know what you are talking about. Mom is just cooking breakfast."

"Well, what in the world is she cooking?"

"Bacon and eggs, I guess."

Must be the bacon, Bud thought.

Bud had never tasted bacon. In fact, he had never eaten any kind of pork. Pork was forbidden by the Mosaic law of the Old Testament. Pap would have a fit if he knew any of his children had eaten it. But it sure smelled good! So when they sat down at the table and the food was passed around, Bud got some bacon, eggs, and toast like everybody else.

Bud knew it was a sin to eat bacon, but he ate it anyway. It sure tasted good!

After breakfast, George and Bud rode their bikes over to Randal Clark's house and played basketball all morning. The goal was just an old bicycle rim nailed to a tree, and the court was just tree roots and dirt. They had a good time anyway playing H-O-R-S-E and one-on-one. Randal was in the same grade as George and Bud, but he was a lot taller than them. Randal was two years older because he had been held back in school twice.

That night, they boys slept in an abandoned junk car in Randal Clark's backyard. It was not all that comfortable, but at least there was no danger of being run over by a train.

Bud woke up with a crick in his neck and a knot in his stomach. They pedaled back up to George's house for some more bacon and eggs. Bud decided he needed to head back to Limp. It was Sunday morning, and he didn't want to go to church with George and his family. He would rather go to the Polebridge Missionary Church with Claire Marie and her family.

Suddenly he realized that he would not make it in time for church. He wondered if Claire Marie would be missing him. "Gotta go, George. See you at school tomorrow!"

"OK, have a nice ride home!"

The trip home was longer and more difficult for some reason. To keep his mind off the long ride, Bud kept thinking about all the fun he had had over the weekend. But he couldn't help but wonder what Mom and Pap would say when he got home. He made it down Claggett Hill and back up the other side with no problem, but Crosier Hill was a different story. Bud ran out of steam about halfway up, near the waterfall ledge, and had to push the bike the rest of the way.

He breathed a sigh of relief when he finally spotted Gilbert and Frances Hay's house at the top of the hill.

When Bud got to Hodge's store, he did not even stop to say hello. Instead, he pedaled down the gravel road and into his own lane in high gear. His back tire slid sideways in the gravel as he made the turn, but Bud didn't even slow down. He parked the three-speed by the woodshed and entered the house through the back door.

Mom was already warming up the pinto beans. Bud could smell fresh cornbread in the oven. "Wash up, Bud. Almost time for lunch."

Mom never even knew I was gone, Bud thought. *No need to let on now.*

Tobacco Harvest

August was coming to an end, and Pap said it was time to cut the tobacco crop and house it in the new barn. Bud was not big enough to cut tobacco, but he was plenty big enough to drop sticks. Pap and the older boys loaded all the tobacco sticks onto the wagon. The tobacco sticks were square cut at the sawmill using lumber left over from the barn build. They were tied with grass strings in square bundles of fifty sticks each. Pap drove along both ends of the tobacco patch and the boys dumped the sticks from the wagon. Bud grabbed all the sticks he could carry and headed down the first outside row, dropping sticks as he counted, "Two, three, two, three, two, three ..."

Once Bud got started on the third row, Jimbo and Hank started cutting the tobacco plants. Five stalks to a stick. Two from this row, three from that one. Then three from this row and two from the other. Pap had made their tobacco knives out of wood stove pokers and sickle blades. They were as sharp as razors. The spears were also handmade, out of brass, with a round, metal file welded to the tip and sharpened to a point. The spear sang out as each stalk of tobacco passed over the flange of the brass spear. When two sticks were filled with tobacco plants, they were leaned against each other for support while the tobacco wilted in the field. By suppertime, half the patch had been cut and Bud had all the sticks dropped. Pap figured they would finish sometime tomorrow afternoon.

And they did.

After allowing the tobacco to wilt in the field for a full day, it was time to house it in the barn. Pap slid a backboard into the brackets on the back of the wagon, and they were good to go! This time, Bud got to drive the tractor, in low gear, while Jimbo and Hank handed the sticks of tobacco up to Pap on the wagon. Pap leaned the tobacco against the backboard, with the tips of the plants touching the floorboards of the wagon. One stick on the left of the wagon. One stick on the right. One in the middle. Two rounds through the tobacco patch, and the wagon was full.

The first load was easy to hang in the barn. Pap just drove the wagon through the back door of the barn and all the way to the front. Hank figured out right away that he wanted the highest tier pole. That way, he would only have to handle every other stick of tobacco. Jimbo was on the lower tier, hanging one stick and handing the next one up to Hank. Bud stayed on the wagon and stood up the sticks for Pap so he didn't have to bend over.

Jimbo and Hank spaced the sticks about ten inches apart on the tier poles to allow room for the air to circulate through the tobacco as it cured. The worst part of Bud's job was the falling tobacco worms that always seemed to land on his head. Tobacco worms are fat and green with spikes rising from their heads and tails. It was hard to tell one end of a tobacco worm from another. Bud thought they were disgusting, but every time he complained about it, Pap would offer to have him trade places with Hank. Bud finally decided that tobacco worms were not so bad after all. Given the choice, he would rather be close to the ground.

A change in procedure was required for the second load. Pap could not drive the tractor through the barn since there were now tobacco plants hanging in the way. Instead, he unhitched the tractor from the front of the wagon and drove around to the back of the wagon. He attached a long push bar from the wagon's back axle to the front bumper of the tractor.

"Here, Bud, lift up the wagon tongue and guide it through the barn, while I push it from behind with the tractor."

Perfect! Bud opened a path through the hanging tobacco and guided the wagon until Hank yelled at Pap to stop. Once the wagon was unloaded, it had to be pushed out of the barn backward and re-hitched to the tractor. Hank decided he was the only one to guide the wagon back out of the barn, since the wagon would be headed downhill once it was out of the barn. It was too big of a job for Bud. So Hank climbed under the hanging tobacco and grabbed the tongue while Jimbo and Bud pushed the wagon back out of the barn.

Jimbo and Bud must have pushed too hard because the wagon backed out of the barn too fast, and down the hill it went! Hank held fast to the tongue with both hands as he chased the wagon. Finally, he managed to turn the tongue and the speeding wagon headed back up the hill. The wagon paused for just a moment and started chasing Hank down the hill. Back and forth they went, taking turns of Hank chasing the wagon and the wagon chasing Hank. Finally, Hank got it stopped, just before they ran into the gully at the bottom of the hill. Pap drove the tractor down the hill, hooked up the wagon, and drove back up the hill. He announced that Jimbo would back the wagon out of the barn for the rest of the day.

Once all the crop was housed in the barn, Pap opened all the barn doors to allow air to circulate through the hanging tobacco.

Halloween Pranks

The first frost came in early October, and Pap sent the boys out with the tractor and trailer to gather all the pumpkins and gooseneck squash from the cornfield. Mom would use the good ones to make pies, and the rest would be cut up for the cows to eat. The boys had two loads piled high with good pumpkins and squash and another load for the cows. Lots of good pies for this winter, and the cows would like them, too! Once the pumpkins and squash were harvested, it was time to pick the corn.

It was Wednesday so Pap and Mom needed to go to Leitchfield for groceries and to Clarkson to visit Aunt Matt. Pap put the three-foot sideboards on the hay wagon to hold the loose ears of corn. He put Jimbo in charge until they got back from town. Pap reminded the boys to get the corn picked and not to be horsing around. That was fine with the boys because that meant they didn't have to stop by Aunt Matt's house. They would rather pick corn all day. Jimbo parked the wagon beside the cornfield, and they headed out into the rows of corn. The boys snapped ears of corn from the stalks with one arm and held them in the other arm. When their arms were full, they dumped the ears into the wagon. They were soon bored so they began to toss the ears of corn at the wagon. Then it turned into a competition to see who could toss an ear into the wagon from the farthest distance. Pap's warning about no horseplay was quickly forgotten.

When they got to the end of the cornfield, Hank declared that he had a better idea. Instead of them being all on the same side of the wagon, why not drive the tractor through the cornfield? They could pick corn from rows on both sides of the wagon at the same time. And Bud could follow behind the wagon to pick up the ears that got knocked over. Soon they had the wagon filled with corn and headed to the crib. The corncrib had a regular door in the front, but it also had a drop-down window that ran the full length of the crib, up near the roof. Jimbo and Hank climbed atop the sideboards of the wagon, unhooked the hinged panel, and let it drop. They unloaded the wagon into the drop-down opening by using scoop shovels.

By the time Pap's Studebaker pulled in the driveway, the wagon was empty and the corncrib was full. "Boys, it's good to see you got all the corn in the crib, because tomorrow we've got another job. Somebody decided to celebrate Halloween a little early and pushed over Mom's outhouse. It is busted up a little. We need to go back to Clarkson tomorrow, repair the outhouse, and set it back up on its foundation.

When they pulled into Aunt Matt's driveway the next

morning with a trunk load of tools, Bud looked around the corner of her house. There was the outhouse, lying on its side. Part of the roof was gone. The front door was broken off at the top hinge.

"This is going to be a stinking mess!" Hank snickered.

"Hush up, boys! The faster we get started, the faster we can finish and get back home."

They lifted the outhouse and moved it to a flat spot in the backyard. Bud could not help but look down into the hole left behind. It was about four feet in diameter and appeared to be fifteen feet deep. It was filled with a stinking brown liquid. Suddenly Bud realized how close the outhouse sat to Aunt Matt's well. No wonder her water tasted funny!

Fortunately, Pap had brought all the tools they needed: extension cords, a Skill saw, squares, a level, new hinges, two bundles of shingles, hammers, and nails. They built a new roof and rehung the front door.

In a couple of hours, they had the outhouse repaired. They stood it back up and scooted it onto its foundation again. It was just a shame that Aunt Matt had no idea who had pushed it over in the first place so she could make them repair the outhouse. Bud and his brothers were just thankful to get the job completed quickly. As Pap backed the Studebaker out of Aunt Matt's driveway, the boys decided to never drink water from her water bucket again.

Lessons Learned

As autumn wore on and the leaves began to change, Bud and Claire Marie went for more walks in the woods. One day they stood under a huge sycamore tree down by the creek and watched the water ripple over the rocks. Bud showed Claire Marie how to skip flat rocks across the surface of the pool upstream from the ripples. Then for some reason, Bud took his Barlow knife out of his pocket and carved a heart into the smooth bark of the sycamore tree. Then another heart.

"What are you doing, Bud?"

"Oh, I don't know."

Bud carved his initials inside one heart and "CME" inside the other. His heart almost leaped out of his chest as Claire Marie traced the initials with her fingertips! And she gazed into his eyes. Suddenly he hoped that Mr. or Mrs. Edmonds never came down that path to the creek.

Bud liked Mrs. Edmonds. She was a good teacher and pretty. Bud was smart, and Mrs. Edmonds often called on him in class. Bud liked that. There were four rows of five desks in

Bud's classroom. Twenty students in all. Claire Marie sat in the front seat of the first row, next to the door to the hallway. Bud sat in the left row of desks, next to the windows. His was the third seat back, behind Hughie Peterson. Hughie wasn't really bright, and Bud had to help him with his schoolwork. That was OK with Bud because he got to impress Claire Marie and her mom with his intelligence.

One morning, Hughie came into class all excited about his dog and her new litter of puppies. They were as cute as could be, but his dad said he couldn't keep them. "My dad says we got to get shed of those puppies! Or else!"

"What did you say?" Mrs. Edmonds turned to face Hughie.

"We got to get shed of those puppies, Mrs. Edmonds!"

Suddenly, Bud realized that Mrs. Edmonds thought Hughie had said a cuss word. Bud spoke up. "No, Mrs. Edmonds. To get shed of something means to get rid of it, like a snake sheds—"

"Be quiet, Bud! Now Hughie Peterson, how exactly do you spell that word?"

"I—I don't know." Hughie stumbled for words, not understanding why his teacher was so upset.

"Well, sound it out. Make a *sh* sound! How do you spell that sound?"

"Sshhh. S-h, I guess."

"That's right. Now what comes after that?"

Bud leaned forward and whispered "e" into Hughie's ear. But for whatever reason, whether he was nervous or just didn't trust Bud, Hughie instead blurted out "I."

"OK, now what is the last letter?" Mrs. Edmonds demanded.

Bud had a lapse in his better judgment, and he just couldn't help himself. "T," he whispered.

"T," said Hughie Peterson. "That's it! S-H-I-T!"

Bud sat up straight, slapped the top of his desk with both hands, and let out a howl of laughter.

"S-H-I-T! Yep, that's it!" Hughie was so proud of himself.

And the entire class was slapping their desks and howling with laughter, just like Bud.

"Bud! Out in the hallway! Now!"

Suddenly the classroom got as quiet as a mouse, and a lump formed in Bud's throat. He followed Mrs. Edmonds out into the hallway.

"Young man, I am *very* disappointed in you! Now march yourself down the hallway to the principal's office and tell Mr. Edmonds what you just did! Now!"

Bud was trying to figure a way out of this mess as he made the long trek to the end of the hallway. He knocked on the office door, and Mrs. VanMeter, the school secretary, opened it. She told Bud to wait as she announced him to Mr. Edmonds.

"What can I do for you, Bud?" Mr. Edmonds asked when he came out.

Bud proceeded to tell Mr. Edmonds what happened.

"Well, Bud, you know I have to punish you for this, right?"

"Yes, sir." Bud noticed the "BOARD of EDUCATION"

hanging by a leather strap on the wall behind Mr. Edmond's desk.

"I am going to give you three licks with the paddle so you will learn from your lesson and think before you do something like this again. Bend over my desk."

Bud stared at the two-by-four hanging on the wall and wondered if he would even survive three licks from that thing. He was relieved to see Mr. Edmonds retrieve a Ping-Pong paddle from the top drawer of his desk. The three licks did sting, but not as bad as Bud had dreaded.

"Now go back to class, Bud. And let this be a lesson to you!"

"Yes, sir."

Instead of going directly back to class, Bud slipped into the bathroom across the hall from the office to calm his nerves. When he came out of the bathroom, the office door was still open. Bud could hear Mr. Edmonds and Mrs. VanMeter chuckling about what had just happened.

Bud opened the classroom door, and all the students stared at him. Except Claire Marie. She was staring down at her desk. Bud was glad it was Friday and close to the end of the day. It was a long bus ride that afternoon. Claire Marie sat beside Bud in the front seat of the bus, but neither said a word all the way home.

Sunday morning came, and the Edmonds family picked up Bud for church, just like any other Sunday. Brother John R. Clark preached about backsliding and how Christian people needed to be careful not to fall back into their old, sinful ways. All Bud could think about was how he had tricked Hughie Peterson into spelling out a cuss word in class. Brother Clark finished his preaching and offered an invitation. Anyone who wanted could come to the altar and pray for forgiveness for backsliding into their old, sinful ways. Bud stepped out into the aisle and began the slow walk to the front of the Polebridge Missionary Church. He was trembling.

Bud kneeled at the altar at the front of the church, closed his eyes, and prayed. He knew what he did was wrong. He did not know what made him do it. Maybe it was the devil. Maybe it was just his sinful nature. Either way, he was a backslider, a sinner, and he needed forgiveness. As he kneeled there and prayed, he felt someone kneel beside him and hold his hand as they began to pray also. It was Claire Marie! Suddenly Bud's spirit was lifted. God had not abandoned him. And neither had Claire Marie!

Black Thread and Pain

Monday morning arrived and Bud was excited to be back in school. Before school started, Bud and George Miller were chasing each other in the hallway. They were not supposed to run in school, but the teachers had not arrived yet, so they would not get in trouble. Over the summer, Western Elementary had been expanded with the addition of a library and two new classrooms at one end of the building. A set of steel double doors that used to be the exterior doors were still in place in the hallway. George ran into the push bar and through one side of those double doors, with Bud tight on his heels. As Bud slipped between the closing doors, his left ear got hung on the metal lock plate. Suddenly, Bud felt an intense pain in his left ear. He touched his ear, and it felt wet!

Bud raced to the bathroom at the other end of the hallway and got a big wad of toilet paper to wipe his ear. He pressed the toilet paper up against his ear, and it throbbed with pain. After holding the tissue in place for a few minutes, Bud removed it and looked into the mirror. That was when he discovered that his ear was nearly cut off! It was attached only by a little bit at the top and a little bit at the bottom. The middle of his ear was cut clean through! Bud hurried to the bathroom stall and got another huge wad of tissue.

About that time, Mr. Edmonds came into the bathroom to see what was going on. George had raced to the office to get help when he saw how badly Bud was hurt. When he saw Mr. Edmonds, Bud just knew he was going to get three licks from the Ping-Pong paddle for running in the hallway. He looked in the mirror at Mr. Edmonds standing behind him. There were wads of toilet paper strewn all over the bathroom floor.

"Here, let me see, Bud." Mr. Edmond's voice was very calm, which surprised Bud. He eased the pressure from the toilet paper compress and examined Bud's ear. "Come on. I need to take you home."

Mom and Pap did not have a phone so there was no way to call them to come get Bud. Claire Marie's dad would have to take Bud home. Bud started crying. His ear was throbbing with each heartbeat. He knew for sure that Pap was going to whip him for running in the hallway and for getting hurt. Bud had never missed a day of school, and that was about to end, too. Bud was simply miserable. It was a long ride from school to Bud's house. Mr. Edmonds explained to Pap what had happened at school and told Pap to take Bud to Dr. Nichol's office in Clarkson to get his ear sewn back on. If Pap could get Bud back to school before the end of the last lunch break, he would not be counted absent.

Pap drove Bud to Clarkson in a hurry. Uncle Chester's

wife, Ollie, worked in Dr. Nichol's office. When Pap and Bud walked in the front door with Bud holding a wad of toilet paper against his left ear, she jumped up from her desk and ran over to look at Bud's ear. Not realizing how badly Bud's ear was cut, she jerked off the paper. Bud almost passed out from the pain. Aunt Ollie ran to the back of the office screaming for Dr. Nichols. Dr. Nichols took one look at Bud's ear and announced to everyone in the waiting area that he had to take care of this emergency. They could stay and wait, or they could leave and come back. No one complained. Dr. Nichols sat Bud in a metal, straight-back chair and told him to grip the rails while he numbed Bud's ear. He then used black thread to stitch Bud's ear back together.

Pap dropped Bud off at Western Elementary's cafeteria door, and Bud ate lunch with the last group of students. When he got back to his fifth grade classroom, all the students gathered around to see his ear and all those black stitches. The rest of the day, the side of Bud's head felt like someone was hitting him with a hammer with every heartbeat. He struggled to hold back the tears because it hurt so bad. After school, Claire Marie and her parents took Bud home so he didn't have to take the bumpy bus ride.

Cold weather was coming, and the woodshed needed to be refilled. Pap hitched up the trailer to the tractor and loaded it with axes, sledgehammers, wedges, the Pioneer chainsaw, gas, and chain bar oil. All the boys piled into the trailer as well, and they headed back to the woods to find firewood. Pap would only saw up dead trees, either standing or on the ground. Dead wood did not need time to cure and was ready for the stove right away. Burning green wood in the stove created a buildup of creosote in the flue and could cause a chimney fire.

As Pap drove down the old log road, the boys scanned the woods for dead trees. Pap stopped when they spotted a good one. Pap used the Pioneer chainsaw to cut a notch on one side of the tree to control its fall, then cut from the back side until the tree started to lean.

"Timber!"

"Wham!"

Bud felt the earth shake when the dead tree hit the ground. Bud's ear was very sensitive to the cold air and had a dull ache most of the time. The impact of the tree jarred his ear and caused it to throb even worse. Pap noticed Bud starting to cry and suggested he take a break until his ear stopped hurting. Hank and Jimbo went right to work using the axes to remove all the limbs. Bud's job was to mark the tree every twenty-four inches, using his hatchet and a stick that Pap had cut to length. Pap followed Bud with the chainsaw, cutting the tree trunk into twenty-four-inch sticks of wood. Jimbo and Hank stacked the wood into the trailer. Soon the trailer was piled high, leaving just enough room for the tools on top.

The boys carried their axes over their shoulders, and they began the long walk back up the hill, out of the woods, and to the woodshed. Bud went inside the house to get some aspirin, hoping the aspirin and the warm stove would ease the pain in his ear. After the wood was unloaded, it had to be split before stacking it in the woodshed.

Working as a team, Pap and the older boys were able to cut, split, and stack about two ricks of firewood each day. In a couple of weekends, the shed was full again and ready for winter.

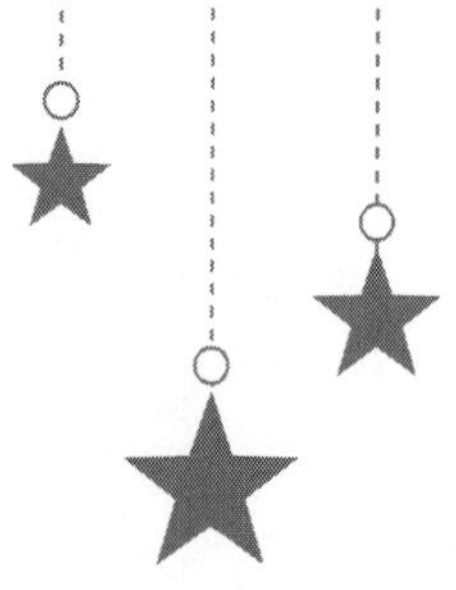

Commodities, Cats, and the U.S. Navy

"I am going to E'town, Bud. Do you want to come along for the ride?" Pap asked Bud one morning.

"Sure, but why do we need to go to E'town instead of Leitchfield?"

"We need to pick up some groceries."

"But we usually do our grocery shopping at Houchen's Market in Leitchfield."

"We are going to the county extension office and pick up a load of commodities."

Bud had no idea what commodities were, but he knew better than to ask any more questions. So he grabbed his coat and climbed into the front seat of the Studebaker, beside Pap. It was a long ride to E'town—a lot longer than the trip to Leitchfield. They passed through East View and Bud recognized George Miller's house down Main Street. At Four Corners, they turned left onto US Highway 62, which was the same road that went to Leitchfield.

Wow, Bud thought. *The same road goes both places!*

Finally, they made it to Elizabethtown and pulled up by a big concrete block building. The sign out front identified the place as "Hardin County Extension Office." Pap and Bud climbed the steps and went inside the office filled with a metal desk and several filing cabinets. There was a picture of the American flag on one wall, and a picture of President Kennedy on another. Bud sat down and examined the room while Pap sat at the desk and filled out a bunch of papers. After they waited about fifteen minutes, a strange man came out and told Pap to back around to the loading dock at the end of the building. There, Pap and Bud loaded box after box into the trunk and back seat of the Studebaker. Bud couldn't wait to get home an open the boxes to see what a commodity really was.

Bud and his brothers helped Pap carry all the boxes into the house and stacked them in the kitchen. Mom began to open them. Powdered milk, powdered eggs, gallon cans of peanut butter, pounds of wrapped butter, and loaves of dark-yellow cheese. Mom cut open a loaf of cheese and gave some to the boys on saltine crackers. The cheese was so soft you could spread it with a butter knife. It was the best cheese Bud had ever tasted.

Wow, he thought. *We sure are lucky to get those commodities! Wherever they came from.*

November arrived. The air was getting drier. The nights were getting colder. The tobacco hanging in the barn was cured and ready for stripping. One evening when the air was damp, Pap and the older boys went to the barn to set up everything for a stripping room. They set up the stripping table, with hanging lights overhead, and plugged in a radio so they could listen to University of Kentucky basketball games on WHAS, 840 AM, on the radio dial.

Hank climbed up into the tier poles and threw down sticks of cured tobacco to Pap and Jimbo, who bulked them into piles. When they had bulked two hundred sticks, they covered the stack with a tarpaulin. The tarp would hold moisture in the tobacco and keep it in "case," which meant the leaves had just enough moisture to be pulled from the stalks without crumbling.

As soon as the boys got home from school the next day, they grabbed a quick bite of supper and headed to the barn to strip tobacco. Jimbo piled ten sticks of tobacco on the right end of the table and got started. Pap always stripped the trash at the bottom of the stalks. Jimbo was next in line, pulling the lugs, or golden leaves, before passing the stalks to Hank on his left. Hank pulled the red leaves and passed the stalks to Bud, who got stuck with the tips. The tips were the shortest leaves at the top of the stalk. Those were the four grades of tobacco: trash, lugs, red leaf, and tips. Not only were the tips the shortest leaves, but they contained the most gum. Within thirty minutes of stripping the tips, Bud's hands were coated with thick, black tobacco gum.

The boys pulled the leaves with the right hand and held the stalk in the left. Once they got a handful of leaves, that "hand" of tobacco was tied by wrapping a long leaf abound the top of the stems and tucking the end of that leaf through the middle of the hand. The hand was then hung straddling an empty tobacco stick. The grades of tobacco were hung on separate sticks. Pap laid out wooden pallets where the sticks of stripped tobacco were stacked until the crop was all stripped and ready for market. The different grades were then loaded on the truck separately. When the truck was unloaded at the tobacco warehouse for sale, each grade was placed on a different flat basket and tagged with the farmer's name, the grade, and the lot number. On sale day, the auctioneer walked through the warehouse basket by basket while the buyers placed their bids and signed the baskets they bought.

The crew usually got stripping tobacco each day around 5:00 and quit around 9:00 in time to get cleaned up for bed. Except when the UK Wildcats were playing a basketball game. On those nights, Pap would turn on the radio and they could listen to the Cats on the radio! Cawood Ledford would interview Coach Adolph Rupp before each game. Coach Rupp had several nicknames: the Baron, Uncle Adolph, and "the man in the brown suit." Coach Rupp always wore a brown suit. Bud loved to listen to Cawood Ledford and Coach Rupp as he described the team's practices as well as what he expected from that night's opponent. Sometimes assistant coach Harry Lancaster would fill in, if the Baron had lost his voice or was busy with last-minute game preparations.

This year's team was nicknamed Rupp's Runts because the tallest player on the team was their center, Thad Jaracz, who was only six feet, five inches tall. Pat Riley, Larry Conley, Louie Dampier, and Tommy Kron also played on the Rupp's Runts team. Bud and his brothers nailed a bicycle rim to the side of the corncrib and played imaginary games when the weather was warm enough, pretending to be Rupp's Runts. Bud's favorite player was Louie Dampier because he was the shortest. Despite playing against teams with much taller players, these Cats were undefeated for much of the year. They ran their plays with precision, sharing the ball with crisp passing and unselfishness. And Cawood Ledford described each play with such colorful language that listening to a UK game on the radio was like having a courtside seat.

As Thanksgiving approached, and in the middle of stripping the tobacco crop, Jimbo announced he was going to join the Navy. Job prospects were tight. Jimbo thought he had a job when he graduated from high school, working at the Ford garage in E'town, but that job fell through. Jimbo knew he did not want to stay on the farm forever. He would have to leave for the Great Lakes Naval Training Station in a week. One of the neighbor boys, Larry Johnson, had enlisted in the Army and had to leave for boot camp at the same time. He agreed to give Jimbo a lift to the Greyhound bus station in Etown so Jimbo could catch the bus bound for Chicago. Bud was excited and proud his big brother Jimbo was joining the Navy. He could not wait to see Jimbo in uniform, with a name badge and medals. Mom was more worried than excited.

The week passed quickly, and the day came for Jimbo to leave. The whole family and most of the neighbors gathered at Bud's house to see Jimbo off and to wish him well. When Larry Johnson's truck pulled into the driveway,

Jimbo already had his suitcase packed, with a new shaving kit inside. Bud sat in the front porch swing, soaking up the moment. Standing on the front porch beside Jimbo was Mom, who was wearing a gingham dress and her tattered apron. Her belly was really getting big. Pap said the baby was due any day now. Bud noticed that Mom was wringing her hands.

Mom's hands were rough, and her fingers were starting to curl from arthritis and milking the cows. Mom's fingernails were short, trimmed at the ends of her fingertips. It was hard to tend a garden with long fingernails. Bud remembered seeing Aunt Effie's hands and how they were smooth with long, painted fingernails. Bud reckoned that Aunt Effie had never milked a cow in her life or tended a garden. She was married to a doctor, and they lived in the city. Bud reached over and squeezed Mom's rough hand. One by one, the neighbors shook Jimbo's hand, patted him on the back, or gave him a hug. As Jimbo loaded his suitcase into the bed of Larry Johnson's truck, Hank went to shake Jimbo's hand and wish him the best. Jimbo put his hand on Hank's shoulder and took a long look into Hank's eyes.

"Hank, you take care of Mom and Pap. And be careful with those bright ideas of yours."

Hank just nodded. He understood that he would have a lot more responsibilities around the farm, with Jimbo gone. Pap stood by the wire yard gate, with his back to the crowd. Tears were running down his cheeks, and he did not want anyone to see. He wondered how he had gotten so old so fast. When he was young, he felt young and he worked like a young man. Until he got hurt. Even as he aged, he still put in a full day's work. Just not as hard. Today he felt old and broken down. His oldest son was off to join the Navy. Things would be different now for sure. *Time slips away,* Pap reckoned. But why did it have to happen so fast?

Finally, it was time to go. Mom hugged Jimbo for the longest time, and they both cried. Pap shook Jimbo's hand and told him how proud he was. And then Jimbo climbed in the front seat, slammed the door, and they were gone. Bud sat in the porch swing and watched the trail of dust out the driveway and down the Salt River Road until they were out of sight. The neighbors said their goodbyes and left. Mom and Pap stood by the front gate, hugging but not saying a word. Bud noticed the chains of the porch swing were squeaking. He had not noticed that before. And he realized they would have to finish stripping the tobacco crop without Jimbo.

Fortunately, Yule Howard came over and helped until they finished. When the tobacco was all stripped and off to market, Bud often sat next to Pap's desk to listen to UK games with him, long after the rest of the family had gone to bed. Pap kept the radio turned down to avoid waking everyone, and Bud kept his ear close to the speaker. Bud always kept a score sheet for each game, recording each shot attempt, goals scored, free throws, rebounds, fouls, and turnovers for both teams. He dreamed of playing for Adolph Rupp and the UK Wildcats when he grew up.

After losing only one game during the regular season, to

the Tennessee Vols, the Cats entered the NCAA tournament ranked number one in all of college basketball. They kept winning. On the night before the national championship game, several of the players came down with a bout of food poisoning, so they were upset by Texas Western. Bud was just as sick as any of the UK players.

Opal in Pink

That Night, Bud heard Mom calling for Pap's help. Her water had broken and they needed to get to the hospital in Leitchfield before the baby was born. Pap warmed up the car and told the boys to get up. Pap told Hank and Bud they would have to get dressed and cook breakfast on their own, because he and Mom were going to the hospital. He told them to come up with a name for the baby. Mom was going to let them pick out her name. Then they were gone. Bud was glad there was no snow on the ground, like the night the Probus baby was born. Bud knew how to cook oatmeal so they had a good breakfast. It was Saturday so they did not have school.

Pap returned later that afternoon with news that their baby sister had been born. Mom and baby would be coming home the next day, but the hospital needed to know what name to put on the birth certificate. Hank reckoned that this baby girl would be the jewel of the family so she needed to be named after a jewel. The boys settled on Opal. Opal

Louise? No, just Opal. No jewel had two names. So Opal it was!

Pap made supper that night. Or at least he tried to make supper. The biscuits were as hard as rocks. Hank did not want to hurt Pap's feelings, so he threw the biscuits out the back door, hoping the dog would eat them. But one bite, and Dusty decided to bury them in the backyard.

The next morning, Pap helped Mom into the house while she carried Opal wrapped in a pink blanket. She told Bud he could hold her if he was careful. Bud sat in the rocking chair and Mom placed Opal in his lap. She was tiny! And cute! With little, pink booties and a pink ribbon in her short hair, she looked up at Bud and smiled. Maybe a baby sister wouldn't be so bad after all! Bud skipped church that week.

A Christmas Present for Claire Marie

Monday morning, Bud talked about his new baby sister all the way to school. And all the way home that afternoon. Claire Marie listened, but her mind was on something else. They were almost to Claire Marie's house when she asked, "What are you going to get me for Christmas?"

Bud hadn't really thought about getting Claire Marie anything for Christmas. After all, his family did not even celebrate Christmas. And they sure didn't give each other Christmas presents. Sure, he had a crush on Claire Marie, and he guessed she probably knew that, but he had not thought anything about Christmas. The question caught him completely off guard. He stammered as the question came out of his mouth. "Well, what would you like for Christmas?"

Bud was trying to buy some time while he gathered his thoughts. He let out a sigh of relief when the bus stopped in front of Claire Marie's house.

She stood up to get off the bus. Halfway down the steps, she turned to Bud. "Oh, I don't know. Surprise me!"

She took a few steps toward the house as Bud stared out the window at her. She turned to look over her shoulder as the bus pulled away. Immediately, Bud went into a panic. He tried to think who he could ask about choosing a Christmas present *for a girl.* He sure could not ask Pap or his mom. Or Hank for that matter. Then Mr. Hodge popped into his head. Yes! He would ask Mr. Hodge!

So when Bud got off the bus, he went straight up to Mr. Hodge's store. Mr. Hodge was behind the counter as usual. Bud was relieved to see there were no customers.

"Mr. Hodge, I need your advice!" Bud began to explain his dilemma.

And Mr. Hodge was very understanding. "I will tell you what, Bud. Look inside this glass display case here on the countertop. These necklaces have tiny gold or silver heart pendants. I bet she would like one of those."

"How much are they?"

"Well, how much do you have?"

"I still have $5 left after buying my bike."

"Perfect! Now would you like a gold one? Or silver?"

Bud picked out a gold one and gave Mr. Hodge the money. Mr. Hodge agreed to hold onto the necklace until Bud came back to pick it up. Bud could not wait for the last day of school before Christmas break.

Finally, the last week of school arrived and Bud rode up to the store to pick up the little box with the necklace inside.

He tucked it inside his coat pocket and carried it around all week at school.

On the last day of school, as they were waiting to get on the bus for the ride home, Claire Marie stood beside Bud and asked him, "Bud, did you get me anything for Christmas?"

"Yes, I did." Bud reached into his coat pocket and pulled out the little velvet box. "Here, open it."

When Claire Marie opened the box, her jaw dropped and her eyes opened wide. She definitely was not expecting this! "It's beautiful! Put it on me please!"

Bud fumbled with his hands as he stood behind Claire Marie and tried to loosen the clasp. Finally, he got it loose, placed the necklace around her neck, and fastened the clasp.

Claire Marie turned to face Bud. "How does it look?"

"Perfect," Bud stammered. And then, before he knew what happened, he kissed her!

And she kissed him back! Softly. Bud heard her make a sound. "Hmmmmmm." Bud opened his eyes and peered deeply into hers. She was crying.

"Bud! You're shaking all over!"

"Yes.... I know."

About the Author

Kenneth R. Powell practices community pharmacy in Bardstown, Kentucky. With a pharmacy career that spans forty-six years, he has been continuously dedicated to improving the health of his patients through accuracy and education. He has personally filled over a million prescriptions during this time but claims his greatest achievement in the dozens of pharmacists and other healthcare professions he has mentored during his career. Through it all, he has impacted the lives of many. During most of his career, Ken has been involved in management at both store and district levels with SupeRx Drugs and Walmart's Pharmacy Division. Nearing the close of his career in pharmacy, Ken is looking forward to different challenges. Fifteen years ago, he and wife Cindy bought a farm in the Washington County community of Willisburg, Kentucky. They raise Black Angus feeder cattle and tend vineyards of both table grapes and wine grapes. You will find wines made from their grapes in several wineries in central Kentucky.